MW01127412

Rainbow Junction

Rainbow Junction

Lowell Harrelson

VANTAGE PRESS
New York

FIRST EDITION

Published by Vantage Press, Inc.
516 West 34th Street, New York, New York 10001

Manufactured in the United States of America
ISBN: 0-533-12909-5

Library of Congress Catalog Card No.: 98-90758

0 9 8 7 6 5 4 3 2 1

Dedicated to the Loving Memory
of
Rebecca Louise Peevy

April 10, 1958—January 20, 1998

"Becky" was my niece, my secretary, my confidante, and best friend. In my heart and mind, Becky was my own dear child. From the day we first met, while she was a toddler, the oldest child of my sister, a special bond began to blossom.

I took great pride in watching Becky develop through high school and then as an Honor Roll Graduate of the University of Southern Mississippi and later earning a master's degree from the University of Houston, again maintaining Honor Roll status throughout.

Desiring a break from her career as a high school music teacher and to fill an urgent need of mine for a secretary, resulted in a working relationship from which we both grew closer than ever.

Being a businessman and secretary was never enough for either of us. We always encouraged each other to go beyond the basics of our training, if for no other reason than the personal enjoyment we would gain by the effort. From such encouragement came this little book.

I had always harbored the desire to record certain childhood experiences within the context of a story and Becky was there to encourage and assist. We knew and accepted the fact that "our" book would not be considered a professional writing and that its value would never be more than the personal pleasure we gained from the effort.

My limited skills left me no choice but to commit every word onto a legal pad, in pencil, during spare time, after hours, or while passing long hours in airports and airplanes.

Becky referred to her role in our partnership as "translation work," a reference to her difficulties associated with trying to decipher my poor handwriting. She occasionally referred to herself as "the editor," suggesting my writing style to be "Classic Lil' Abner."

Within a few short months after our completion of this venture into "activities beyond our abilities," Becky was diagnosed with terminal cancer. The disease brought Becky such pain and discomfort as to render her last nine months after diagnosis almost unbearable.

Becky quietly passed out of this world on the evening of January 20, 1998, again displaying her consistent regard for accommodating my schedule by allowing the time for me to make my usual bedside visit after closing my office. I was there, along with her immediate family, during those agonizing last minutes of Becky's life. As we consoled each other, I recalled some of my conversations with Becky about how we should never fear the unknowns we encounter but rather we should always venture into each with optimistic expectations. Those memories did serve to soften the loss I was feeling.

Becky is no longer with us, but her memory will exist with me forever. Reading our book is painful for me because every page contains some word or sentence that revives some recollection of her "editing comments." I am told that "time will heal all wounds." For me that will require a very long time.

ONE

"There it is, folks, the most beautiful village in America! Rainbow Junction, Alabama. The onliest spot on Earth that mighta been better wuz the Garden of Eden and God kept that for Him and Adam and Eve."

We looked down on that little town from the top of Sand Mountain. There state highway 103 provides a wide shoulder large enough to accommodate the parking of Deacon Johnson's 1949 one-and-a-half ton, stake-bodied Dodge truck. It was a magnificent sight for my eleven year-old eyes to behold.

Deacon Johnson was prancing around all of us standing in front of his truck, looking down on that little town. He was ranting on as if he had been vaccinated with a phonograph needle. The way he carried on, I thought heaven itself was just down the hill.

Deacon Johnson's full name was J.D. Johnson. He told us that when he first came to visit us over a month ago. He never said what the "J.D." stood for and we didn't ask since lots of men in Alabama have "first names" of simple initials.

One thing for sure, Mr. J.D. Johnson was a big man. As he stood in front of us, I couldn't help noticing his stomach hanging out over his belt. He was at least twice the size of my daddy and the big boots he had on made him look taller than Daddy. His weathered khaki trousers and shirt seemed to blend well with his equally weathered face and hands. He removed a grayish felt hat, revealing a head with little hair except a line just above his ears. He kept a friendly smile on

1

his face that made our family feel very comfortable in his presence. Momma said it was like the deacon has adopted us. First he led the search committee that invited Daddy to become their new preacher. Now he had volunteered his services and that of his truck to get us moved.

The deacon was busy explaining all the wonderful things he could think to tell about our new hometown. He didn't notice how anxious Daddy, Momma, Evelyn, and I were to get on down the mountain. We were ready to unload our belongings off his truck and into our new home, which was the parsonage of the First Baptist Church of Rainbow Junction.

We all remained patient. Everybody except me pretended to show great interest. The deacon lapsed into describing the high points of interest in the town that lay some seven to ten miles below and east of where we stood. "The white building in the center of town is the courthouse," he said. "Now, if you look hard about three blocks behind the courthouse going farther away, you can see the First Baptist Church. The reverend here will deliver many fine sermons there in days to come."

I wished to become better acquainted with a king-sized Sand Mountain toad frog I had spotted from the corner of my eye. I was standing between, but slightly in back of Momma and Daddy. My body was preparing a surprise leap in the direction of the frog. Then Momma's downward glance sent a message of correction deep into my soul. Momma could always send strong messages with her eyes the way Daddy did with throat sounds. I never understood how this form of communication developed. I can promise it worked. Failure on my part to identify the directions intended for me in Momma's stare or Daddy's throat sounds always resulted in my discomfort.

I straightened up, put on my best Sunday school smile,

and moved a little forward as if to show my greater interest. I glimpsed my sister Evelyn poised like the little angel that she always appeared to be. She was squarely in front of Momma, peering out in the direction of Deacon Johnson's projected finger. She had an expression like one might expect from the lost children of Israel as Moses pointed toward the opened sea.

Barely catching his breath, Deacon Johnson continued, "Off to your far right, you can see the mighty Coosa River coming down from north Georgia right past our little town. The Coosa is headed toward joining up with the Alabama River down close to Montgomery. Now looking almost straight ahead, but a little off to your left, you see the big Tallapoosa Creek. It's flowing southward till it meets the river just this side of town."

After another deep breath, which I noticed caused a low-toned kinda snort, Deacon Johnson reached the climactic point in his long-winded praises to his old hometown. "There, now you can see exactly how our great town got its name. Many days during the year, especially in the summer when the storms blow in, the clouds produce heavy rains. The minute the rain stops, great rainbows appear in the sky. From up here on Sand Mountain, it always looks just like one end of every one of those rainbows settles down in the middle of the Coosa River off to your right. The other end always looks like it comes right out of big Tallapoosa Creek down yonder on the left. Now you tell me, how in God's name any town sittin' under a rainbow going from creek to river could ever be named anything but Rainbow Junction!"

"Amen," said Daddy.

"Praise the Lord," said Momma.

"It's beautiful," said sister Evelyn, and I said, "I'm gettin' hungry. My belly's startin' to growl."

We were back in Deacon Johnson's old truck, easing

3

back on to the highway, making our way toward the new parsonage that I was anxious to explore. Daddy, Momma, and sister Evelyn were all squeezed into the cab of the old truck with Deacon Johnson. I maintained my vigil amongst the furniture stashed to the top of the stake body in the back.

I stood up in the back of the truck for the balance of the trip. By placing my feet between two of the slats of the truck body, I was able to get my head high enough to see everything. The wind in my face felt good. I was trying to look both ways at once. We picked up speed going those last miles down the mountain. We crossed the bridge over big Tallapoosa Creek. The town looked lots smaller than Birmingham. It struck me as being just like some other towns that we passed on our way here.

I already liked my new hometown. I felt a surge of excitement just thinking about all the new things I might find here.

The streets were lined with trees on both sides. The buildings looked good to me, even though Deacon Johnson had called the town an old town.

I saw the big white courthouse building that Deacon Johnson had pointed out when we stopped on the mountain. I remembered him saying the church and parsonage were right behind the courthouse.

Suddenly I felt my first tinge of sadness about the home and friends that we were leaving behind. Up until this hot day of May 1954, three days after school let out for the year, my entire life had been lived in the parsonage of the Shady Grove Baptist Church just outside Birmingham, Alabama.

My daddy, the Reverend John Preston Williams, had been the pastor of the Shady Grove Baptist Church for fifteen years. Beginning the day he completed his studies at the Baptist seminary, he was "called," as the Baptists say, to become the pastor of that church. I heard him and my momma tell about how scared he was to suddenly show up in that little church of a hundred or so, mostly older folks, and start preaching the gospel. They both talked about how shy he was. He must not have been too shy since he married my momma, who played the church piano, within six months after he became the pastor. A little more than a year after they were married, "God sent them their angel Evelyn." Just over a year later, I was born. Evelyn was now coming up on her thirteenth birthday. I had turned eleven two weeks before we left Shady Grove.

I might have been partial, but I believed my daddy was a perfect man. He was tall enough but not too tall. He was thin but not too thin. He always wore clean white shirts even though some of them looked worn-out at their collar. Daddy seldom talked without addressing something important. Idle chatter just wasn't his style. I could tell he's real proud of me. I even heard him say that sometimes.

Daddy believed in teaching by example. He said, "Yes, sir" and "No, sir" or "Yes, Ma'am" and "No, Ma'am" to all his elders just like he expected from me and Sister Evelyn. He always wore a hat when outdoors but never a cap, which he said makes him look lazy.

I knew Daddy worked hard at being a good preacher. Sometimes I thought he felt like he was the only thing standing between a world full of sinners and a hell full of fire and brimstone. The thing I liked best about Daddy was the way he listened to everything I told him.

Baptist preachers have a way of being "called" to bigger congregations. This was our big call, going to the First Baptist Church of Rainbow Junction.

Before she married Daddy, my momma was Betty Mae Johnson. No kin to Deacon Johnson, it's just that Alabama has lots of Johnsons. I can't say for sure, but I believe my momma had played the piano all her life. She kept playing the church piano after she married Daddy. When I got old enough to leave the church nursery and sit on a church pew, she would play the piano during the song service, then come sit between me and sister Evelyn while Daddy preached. My momma was the sweetest, kindest, and best-liked lady in the whole world. She also knew secret ways to apply pain when I didn't "do what is right." She had been known to place a heavy pinch on the thigh of my leg for a minor provocation. Sometimes her pinch left a "blue spot" that took weeks to wear off.

In my mind, my momma was the perfect match for Daddy. She's a little shorter and more likely to point out things that Daddy would never notice. She was always re-minding him to comb his hair after he took his hat off when we get to church.

Momma sometimes reminded Daddy that his brown hair was showing some gray at the edges. Her hair was still shiny black the way it's always been. If Momma had a flaw, it was being too thin. Daddy sometimes told her not to go outside on a windy day without a brick in her hand or the wind might blow her away.

Momma's eyes were almost as dark as her hair. She mostly always smiled until she caught me doing or even thinking something I shouldn't. Then her eyes kinda squinted and she stared at me in a way that made me feel like her eyes were darts.

Except for being perfect, there ain't much to say about sister Evelyn. She always smiled, picked up her clothes, and made straight A's. According to Momma, she was exactly what a young Southern Christian lady should be. Every-body said Evelyn was "the spittin' image" of Momma.

TWO

Thank God we're here! Deacon Johnson backed the truck up to the front porch. Members of the church and some neighbors gathered round to help unload our belongings. Momma directed every move. Sister Evelyn wanted her bed against the window. Daddy wanted to walk over to the church. I couldn't wait to talk to the girl on the bicycle who kept pedaling up and down the street in front of our new house.

Daddy talked to me about not being scared the first night in our new home. He said a prayer, turned off the light, closed the door, and left me to deal with whatever I felt, saw, or imagined. It was darker here than it was in Shady Grove. There were sounds here I'd never heard before. This room was full of bugs and maybe some spiders thrown in for good measure. I heard a loud bump under the house. Could that be an alligator? We were now living between a creek and a river—that sure could be an alligator. I believe I remembered Deacon Johnson saying something about gators not living this far north. I sure hoped that was right. One more bump and I was gone. I'd try saying my prayer so maybe I'd sleep. "Please, God, let daylight come so I can get started in this new place."

A brand new day, lots of sunshine, a fresh new start, and I was ready. Folks all over the place, helping Momma move things from place to place around the house. Washing dishes, making beds, all talking at the same time. It was time for me to look this place over.

I remembered what Deacon Johnson said after he had

backed the truck up to the front porch. "If you go that way, west on this street, it takes you all the way to the creek. Go east and it ends at the river."

I went west toward the creek, figuring I should examine the smaller body of water first and then go see the river. I crossed several streets, noticing nothing of particular interest. My bare feet felt a little uncomfortable as the morning sun heated the pavement. I kept walking faster and faster past the stockyard, over the railroad tracks, and finally arriving at my destination. The sight of the Big Tallapoosa Creek, whose muddy waters swirled past, gave me my first encounter with the magic derived from the observation of floating objects headed to points unknown.

I don't know how long I had stood motionless staring at the creek waters before I was startled by a voice. It sounded like it came from someone my age who said, "What's your name?" I located the source of the question holding a cane pole, squatting in the mud a few feet upstream from where I stood. I replied, "My name is John Preston Williams, Junior. I just moved into the parsonage of the First Baptist Church yesterday with my daddy, the preacher, and my momma and sister. What's your name?"

"My name is Telfair Dedeaux. You spell that D-E-D-E-A-U-X. Folks round here don't never know how to spell my name 'cause I'm from Louisiana. My papa moved us here last year so he could work on the new river bridge. Some folks calls us Cajuns."

"Well, Mr. Telfair Dedeaux," I said but he interrupted, "No. I told you that was my name, but Papa calls me Skeeter, so's everybody else calls me Skeeter, too."

"Okay, Skeeter, then tell me, what's a Cajun?" I said.

"I don't know," he replied, "but I reckon it's somebody from Louisiana with a different kinda name. Maybe it's 'cause we eat crawfish and whup alligators."

"I'll just call you Skeeter, too," I said.

"Fine with me," said Skeeter. "What'll I call you?"

"Daddy started calling me Junior the day I was borned and everybody else does, too," I said. "Watchya doin', Skeeter?" I said, trying to be friendly and keep the conversation going.

"Any fool could see I'm fishin'," he said, as if addressing a complete idiot.

"I ain't never been fishin' 'cause there ain't no creeks in Birmingham," I replied.

I can't begin to describe the thrill I felt when Skeeter next said, "Come on over here and squat down next to me, and I'll show you how it's done. If you show good sense and stay real quiet, I might let you pull the next one out."

With that invite, I moved in the direction of Skeeter Dedeaux. He was perched there on the creek bank like a giant bullfrog. I began to explore a brand new world previously unknown to me. With every step toward the spot occupied by Skeeter, I felt the ooze of the soft mud of the creek bank between my toes. At first, the mud felt slimy and each step was taken slowly. The more steps I took, the better the mud felt to my feet and toes. By the time I came to a stop next to Skeeter, I had discovered one of life's greatest pleasures, that being the feel of cool mud oozing up between the toes and over the bare feet. With this, I couldn't imagine ever wearing shoes again.

I squatted next to Skeeter, resting my buttocks on the back of the calves of my legs, just like him. Then I settled in for my first lesson on fishing with the intensity of one being instructed in the art of heart surgery.

"Don't take your eye off the bobber," was his first admonition. "You can hold the pole with both hands or just one, either way you like. Make sure you're ready when a big catfish comes a-callin'. Ever now and 'n, you raise the pole high enough to get your hook outa water so's to see if the worm's still on. Like that," he said. "Sometimes them little bitty bream will ease up to your hook and take your worm without even makin' that bobber move. Just watch me for a while and you can be a expert like me in no time."

Skeeter finished his lesson on fishing, which I absorbed the way a starving dog eats leftovers. Then I had to satisfy my curiosity about my newfound friend.

"How old are you, Skeeter?" I asked.

"I'm ten right now, but come August sometime, I'll be eleven."

"We're 'bout the same," I said, "I'm eleven already. What grade'll you be in when school starts back?"

"Third," he said, showing some noticeable concern for my line of questioning.

"Third," I exclaimed. "You and me 'bout the same age, but I'll be goin' to the sixth and you to the third. How come that?"

With that, Skeeter opened up and within a few minutes had set my mind at ease about who he was and why he was still at the third-grade level. He told about how his ma had died when he was born. He lived with his pa in a small camper trailer that his pa pulled behind his pick-up truck. His pa was a construction worker who moved from job to job. He also talked about how he didn't much like going to school because teachers ask dumb questions. Him and his pa didn't stay in one place very long and, besides, fishing was a lot more fun.

By the time he had finished telling me about himself, he was laying on his back against the mud. He was looking up at the sky while holding the pole balanced between the toes of his right foot.

"Looky here," he said, "if you lay back like me and stare hard at them white fluffy clouds sailin' by up yonder, then raise up real quick lookin' at the water goin' by, it'll make you dizzy. Then you'll feel funny."

I tried what he suggested several times. Sure enough it did make me dizzy and I did feel funny. For a minute I thought I was learning more in one day than I had learned my whole life. I felt that, in that brief time on the creek bank, I had grown several inches taller and immensely wiser.

"Do ya ever catch anything?" I inquired. With that question, Skeeter leapt to his feet. I immediately noticed he was taller than I was. He had dark hair that seemed to grow in all directions and hadn't been cut for weeks. He pulled a short iron rod out of the mud, which had gone unnoticed by me. By pulling in a long string attached to the rod, he flashed his catch of that day. I couldn't believe my eyes. He had three big catfish and two bream secured by the string that ran through their gills and out their mouths. I had never seen that many fish before, especially alive. I touched them all, watched them flap around on the string and marveled at the abilities of this newfound friend.

"I gotta go," said Skeeter. "My pa gets to the trailer 'fore dark and I'll have these fish cleaned so's he can pop 'em in a pan for supper fer us. Meet me back here tomorrow, early, and I'll bring another pole so you can fish too. We might go further up the creek towards the grist mill. Maybe we'll meet up with Willie. Willie's a nigger 'bout."

"Stop!" I screamed. "Don't ever use that word. My daddy says that's a vile word never to be used. It makes colored folks mad. Besides, it ain't right for Christian people to speak words that riles other folks up. What you s'posed to say when talking 'bout black folk is Nee-grow or colored, but never, never, never that word you jest said."

Skeeter stared at me for a while with a look of confusion. He wasn't fully understanding my concern for his remarks. Not wishing to end our new friendship after barely

11

getting started, he continued. "Maybe if you brought yo'self down here early in the mornin' we could do some fishin'. We might walk this creek bank on up yonder close to the grist mill. We might meet up with Willie who's 'bout as good as me at fishin'. Then you can see for yo'self that Willie's a Nee-grow or colored or whatever you think, which don't matter none to me. Willie says a Cajun and a nig—'scuse me, Nee-grow, goes good together. All I know is Willie knows more good fishin' holes than anybody 'cept his Uncle Winslow and I like to find all the good fishin' holes in this creek."

With that, Skeeter was running down the creek bank toward the trees down by the railroad. That's where house trailers were scattered around at all different angles, as though they were dropped from the sky and left to float like feathers into whatever place they landed.

Now realizing that my first day in my new hometown was quickly fading into history, I retreated back down the creek bank. I soon found my way onto the pavement of Fourth Street where it ended at the creek. I immediately turned eastward, which would land me safely back at home after about one mile. Trotting along Fourth Street on my way back, I crossed back over the railroad tracks. Again I saw and smelled the stockyards on the north side of the street. I added a little speed to my trot in order to assure arrival before sundown.

Beginning to trot even faster while filling my head with visions of whopper catfish I would soon be taking from the big Tallapoosa Creek, I could now see the oak trees several hundred yards away that signaled my arrival into our neighborhood. For a brief moment, the thoughts of big catfish cleared out of my mind at the sign of that same girl whom I saw yesterday while moving into the parsonage.

She was gracefully pedaling her bicycle down the street toward me.

Just as I came to the corner of our front yard, the girl on the bicycle passed right by me, going the opposite way. She was sitting coolly on the seat of her bike, with her long blond hair waving gently behind her. I felt a burst of energy big enough to propel old Deacon Johnson's truck all the way back to Birmingham. With that, I moved into the fastest run of my life. I turned into our front yard, going between the side of the house and the fence that divided our yard from our neighbors, skidding up to our back porch totally exhausted.

I came to a stop at the edge of our back porch and was suddenly aware of being the object of three sets of eyes from the three people standing at the edge of the porch. Their stares alerted me of an impending crisis. They took turns speaking.

From Sister, who spoke first, came the anticipated conveyance of disgust. "You are a muddy mess."

Then Momma, "Where on Earth have you been all day?"

And finally my daddy, in a more acceptable tone, said, "Get yourself cleaned up. Supper's ready and afterward you and I will sit for a while out here on the back porch."

Getting cleaned up in that old four-legged bathtub, leaving behind enough mud to half-fill a wheelbarrow didn't take much time. Daddy asked the blessing on the evening meal. The food was consumed amidst small talk, throat sounds, and stares. Afterward, I met Daddy on the back porch for that time he always called "sitting together."

I sat in a straight-backed chair across from Daddy in his big rocker for what seemed like hours. We listened only to the sound of crickets and frogs. I was shocked at the tone of his voice when he finally spoke out.

"Now, Son," he said, "I know you are now eleven years old. I know we now live in new surroundings with much to explore and your nature is to fully explore. I also recognize that this new place affords you opportunities to experience new adventure. All of this I accept within the limits of exercising good judgment and a sense of responsibility on your part."

As my daddy continued to talk, I could sense for the first time in my life an acceptance by him of my being a person in my own right, with fears and desires to be acknowledged.

After a short pause, Daddy continued his remarks, beginning with, "Now always keep in mind your momma's tendency to worry and don't strain her nerves too much."

"Yessir," I said.

"Also, I should remind you to be more considerate of your sister, who is sometimes prone to embarrassment by your actions."

I mumbled something sufficient to be taken for "yes, sir" while wishing I could say I couldn't care less what Sister thought.

Then in a tone of voice I might have expected from one of the Bible prophets, Daddy got to the most serious part of our discussion. "You must always remember that your father is a minister. I know that will sometimes work to your disadvantage. I was called of God at age thirteen to serve Him for life in the preaching of His gospel. You also know that I pray every day that should God also decide to call you as He called me, your conscience will permit you to answer Him back as I did. That answer was that I was ready."

While I was responding with words to the effect that I understood his interest in my future, I was thinking how the only calling I had got so far was that creek, those catfish,

14

Skeeter with his fishing pole, and maybe a whisper from the girl on the bicycle.

When the crickets and frogs had completed several more of their renditions of night music while Momma and Sister were cleaning the kitchen, I got up the nerve to raise a few issues of my own. "Daddy," I asked, "what's a Cajun from Louisiana? I met a feller down by the creek today that showed me how to fish and said he was a Cajun. He said he come here with his papa from Louisiana. He said his last name was 'Dee-Doe,' but you spell it D-e-d-e-a-u-x."

"*Cajun* is a slang word used by some people to designate folks down in Louisiana who come from French descendants. Don't use that word and try not to ever use any word about any people or person if the word in question has any chance of offending them."

"Yessir!" I said loudly and then rattled on as long as Daddy would listen about Skeeter and all the things he told me and all the things he was going to teach me. Daddy was patient through my dissertation of the merits of my future plans with Skeeter, though occasionally raising an eyebrow at some particular comment. With a grunt that said it was bedtime, we went to our rooms. I said my prayers, asking God's safekeeping for all, especially Skeeter. I now needed him for future instruction. Sleep came easy with no thoughts about spiders or gators and no bumps from beneath the house.

THREE

I couldn't believe my eyes. The sun was already peeking over the chinaberry tree in the backyard, clearly visible from my bedroom next to the back porch. Skeeter had said to meet him early. I gobbled down two biscuits left on the table and rolled the britches legs of my overalls up to my knees. Momma talked about being careful and then I ran as fast as my feet would carry me back to the west end of Fourth Street where it ended at the creek.

There he was, standing about where I first saw him yesterday. Skeeter was visibly impatient, holding two cane poles and two cans of worms. Before I could think of what to say, Skeeter spoke first. "Good afternoon, preacher boy. Did you get your beauty rest?" Even with the flash of anger I got from his remark, I still couldn't get a word in before he continued. "I did say to be here early, didn't I?" he said with a smirk. Then to my further disgrace, he added, "Now remember this, preacher boy, if you plan to run with the big dogs, you'll have to learn to pee in tall grass." I was flabbergasted! "Preacher boy"—I hate that phrase. Doing this unmentionable in tall grass. What's this world coming to? The good side is I will have been here two full days after today and will have been fishing twice. Surely this must be what heaven was like. I heard my daddy preach many times about heaven being whatever makes us happiest on Earth. I'd just traipse along here behind Skeeter, looking for the fishing hole that he says holds the "Grandaddy-of-them-all" and figure I'm already in heaven. That sure made me feel good, being in heaven without all the pain of dying, which was the one thing that'd always troubled me about going to heaven.

"How much farther to the good fishin' hole?" I inquired of Skeeter. "I must have ten pounds of mud on each foot. Some of them worms are beginning to stick their heads over the top of the can."

"Shut up and come on," replied Skeeter, with the same contempt he had shown at my presence when we first met up this morning.

I continued my tramping through the mud some four or five feet behind Skeeter, holding my cane pole in one hand and the can of big crawler worms in the other while perspiration dripped from the end of my nose.

I decided to count the drops of sweat falling off my nose. I was ignoring the angle of the cane pole in my left hand until it came to rest squarely between the legs of Skeeter when he stopped to check on my condition. Mistaking the feel of my cane pole against the upper inside of his legs for a snake or some varmint of unknown origin, Skeeter yelled a jumble of words that shocked me to the point of my falling backwards into a mud hole. As my bottom side hit in the mud hole, it triggered a response that must have been lingering in my subconscious mind. Having never expressed such a reaction before, I exclaimed with bitterness, "Ah, shit!" Then realizing the awfulness of my choice of words, I quickly jumped to my feet, looked at Skeeter, and said in a voice that could be heard across the creek, "Oh, God, you made me say 'shit.' " With exasperation setting in and realizing I had said "shit" and "God" in the same sentence, I then said, "The hell with it. I'll sit down right here and fish."

Some amount of time passed, with me sitting there with my pole extended out over the edge of the creek, my hook three feet under water with neither of us speaking until Skeeter demonstrated remarkable understanding. He spoke up, saying, "While you sit there trying to decide if the devil is comin' for you tonight, you might as well put a worm on your hook just in case a fish comes by."

Daddy always said that laughter cures a multitude of problems. It worked for Skeeter and me. Within a few minutes, we were making our way farther up the creek bank in the direction of the grist mill. We had more mud on our feet than I could have carried in a sack.

"Hey, y'all down yonder!" another voice from afar, I thought. Sure enough, I looked up toward the top of the rise just beyond the creek bank looking back toward town and there he stood. He was waving his arms to get our attention. "That's him," said Skeeter. "That's Willie I been tellin' ya 'bout. Willie knows ever' good fishin' home in this here creek. He learnt 'em all from his Uncle Winslow 'fore his uncle got too old to fish." Willie was already halfway down the hill, running full speed, coming toward us when I noticed his cane pole in one hand and his worm can in the other.

Willie was suddenly standing next to us after sliding down the ten feet or so of the creek bank. He came to rest at the water's edge where Skeeter and I were waiting.

"Looks like we all ready to see what fish is waitin' out there to jump up on deese hooks," Willie said, with the biggest grin I had ever seen.

"We ready to go," said Skeeter. "We already late 'cause preacher boy here had to get his beauty sleep."

"What you mean, preacher boy?" asked Willie.

"Ah, we ain't got time for all that right now," shot back Skeeter. "What's we need right now is to find the hole where the most fish lives."

Obviously proud of the respect for leadership being shown by Skeeter, Willie quickly outlined our plan. "First

18

we walk on up to the grist mill. Then we walk out on the top of the dam where the water backs up to feed the water wheel. We den takes the old log foot bridge from the end of the dam over to da other side of da creek. We go up the other side a little ways to where Devil's Slue comes into da creek. We den go up da slue a little ways to da deep holes in da slue and da fish is der in droves."

"What's a slue?" I asked.

"Man, you axe more questions than anybody," said Skeeter. "You must not know nothin'. A slue ain't nothing more'n a big old ditch that runs into the creek. Mostly it ain't got but a trickle o'water goin' through till it rains, then it fills up real deep and the fish think they got a new home. Once they in, the water runs off to the creek, leavin' them back there in the deep holes."

"Yeah," Willie chimed in. "Sometimes dey so many fish in a hole you can 'mos' picks dem up wit' yo' hands."

We moved up the creek bank. We came to the grist mill pond dam and walked on out to the end. The log footbridge allowed us safe passage across the other half of the creek on to the creek bank on the other side of big Tallapoosa Creek. Another few yards farther up the creek bank on the west side, we came to a wide ditch flowing into the creek that Skeeter and Willie said was the Devil's Slue. I sure did want to inquire as to how it got its evil-sounding name, but time and my reluctance to demonstrate further ignorance kept me quiet. Following Willie in front and Skeeter right behind him, we headed west on the banks of the slue. I reckoned it got its awful name from the fact that it was coming out of the swamp up ahead and was mostly covered over by trees, vines, and weeds that got worse the farther we went.

I was about to show my lack of ability for enduring such a trip when Willie finally stopped. He raised his right hand holding his worm can and said, "Dis is de bes' hole I know of fer us to start wif." The hole he pointed to was almost round like a big tub. The sandy edge around the hole provided a good place for sitting down to fish. There was a little clearance of trees and vines around one side of the hole on the side where we were walking. It did look to me like a perfect spot.

It wasn't long before I had three bream and a catfish. I had to divide my fish on Skeeter and Willie's stringer line since I had been "too stupid," according to Skeeter, to bring my own. "I'll bring you a pole and worms till you get one for yo'self," said Skeeter, "but I'll be damned if I'm gonna furnish you a stringer to take 'em home with."

I felt a strong urge to correct the bad language of Skeeter that I was totally against, but I figured it was just his way and anything I said now might make bad matters worse.

Anyhow, Willie caught four big catfish and Skeeter caught something called a "grinnel." I hadn't ever heard of a grinnel, but it looked kinda like a big black catfish that snorted like a small pig when Skeeter pulled it out on the sand and held it down with his foot to get the hook out of its mouth.

I found out later that most folks don't eat grinnels, but Skeeter said, "Cajuns eats anything what don't eat them first."

There musta been a thousand of every kind of bird in the world livin' down in the swamp. Every time we got quiet when Willie said "We's botherin' the fish," I could hear all them birds hollering their lungs out at the same time.

I listened to see if I could make out what they were trying to say. I couldn't. There were those that chirped, some that peeped, others that whistled, a few that make knocking sounds like people do when they come to your door and there were some that sounded downright scary. They sounded to me just like that old lady's cat back at Shady Grove when Momma took me with her to visit the old lady and I accidentally sat down in her rockin' chair and rocked on her cat's tail.

When the fish stopped biting and things got quiet, I'd try different conversations. I demonstrated my knowledge of the Bible with a few Scriptures I'd learned in Sunday school. Willie said he knowed a Bible verse too. Then he quoted John 3:16: "For God so loved the world." I had to help a little, but he was proud when he finished. He said his granny had read him Scriptures sometimes like Daddy does for me.

Skeeter didn't like being the only one who didn't know a Bible verse. When he stood up to stretch his legs, he recited one his pa had taught him. He said, "Yea, tho' I walk through the valley of death, I will not fear, 'cause I ain't scared o' nobody." Skeeter said King David had said that. I thought it sounded a little familiar. I didn't ask Skeeter anymore about the verse that his daddy had taught him. It did sound like something King David would say. After all, he was the boy who had killed a giant with a slingshot. I liked King David.

By now the sun had moved over to the downhill side of the day. The fish had quit biting and my belly was starting to growl the way it always does when I don't eat on time. "I'm hungry," I said. "Stop whining," said Skeeter. "Ain't nuttin' out chere to eat," Willie said. So I just sat there, wishing I had brought the leftover biscuits that Momma had baked for breakfast.

As if to impress me with his vast knowledge of the great outdoors or maybe to increase my agony by reminding me of food, Willie lit into telling how people get by when out in the woods without food.

"Der's some fine scuppernong vines on a big oak tree a little farther up towards the swamp," said Willie. "Dey do give some fine eatin' scuppernongs, but dey don't get ripe till August. Den," he confided, "deys a big crabapple tree jes' out yonder, but dey ain't ripe yet neither and if you eat 'em green, dey makes you squirt like a goose."

For the sake of something better to do and to get my mind off eating or maybe to satisfy my natural curiosity, I decided to find out more about Willie.

"How old are you and what grade you goin' to be in when school starts back?" I asked. Before Willie could answer, Skeeter jumped to his feet, looking right at me with his face kinda red and said, "You might as well tell him everything you can think of, Willie. I swear this preacher boy axes more questions than most folks can answer."

I couldn't figure why Skeeter got mad at my questions. I figured it had something to do with his being from Louisiana. Willie didn't seem to mind, as he laid out all about himself for me.

Sounding a little bit like somebody registering with his draft board, Willie began to explain. "I'll be twelve years old on this comin' Christmas Day. I live with my grandma and I ain't never even seen my pa. My mamma left for a job in Detroit when I was real little, and I don't see her much 'cept at Christmas. I'll be in de fiff grade when school starts back up, if'n I go. I goes to de Booker T. Washington School dat ain't nowhere close to where de white chillun goes." After that, we all three sat silent for some time, watching our bobbers in the fishing hole.

I was impressed with the fact that Willie was bigger than me or Skeeter. When he smiled, which was most of the time, his teeth reminded me of Momma's simulated pearls she wore with her black funeral dress. Daddy sometimes re-

22

ferred to some friend of his as a "man's kind of man." That's how I felt about Willie.

I also learned that Willie's last name was Baines. His daddy was from Birmingham. He had come to town working on a tugboat. Willie got to sounding real sad, telling about how his daddy had drowned after falling off the boat. The drowning occurred just before he was born and his mother had to go up North to find a job.

"What ya'll learn at the Booker T. Washington School?" I asked Willie, showing my curiosity not yet satisfied.

"Readin', ritin', and 'rifmatic," said Willie, "jes' like everbody."

"What's two plus two at Booker T. Washington School?" I pursued of Willie. "Fo'!" he exclaimed as if he had just won the stand up arithmetic test at school.

"Whatya know," I said. "That's same as it is at the Shady Grove School where I been goin'. You sure are smarter than any boy I knowed at Shady Grove. Wonder why we goin' to different schools?"

That hit Skeeter's boiling point. "Talk, talk, talk," said Skeeter. "That's all you want to do. You probably done run the fish to the next county. Anyhow, it's gettin' late and they ain't bitin' here no more, so's Willie needs to find us another hole."

Willie stood up, surveyed the situation and explained how we couldn't move on up the slue, staying along its banks because the heavy vines had us blocked. Willie explained how we had to move away from the slue out towards the deep woods. We had to get around the heavy vines, then come back to the slue after we had negotiated our detour.

Off we went again. Willie in front, Skeeter right behind him, and me in back, lugging my pole, worm can, and Skeeter's stringer with his big grinnel and my fish.

23

It seemed like we had been walking around trying to get back to the slue for hours, dodging trees, stumps, limbs, and untangling ourselves from vines before Willie stopped. With some degree of anguish, he announced to Skeeter and me, "We is sho-nuff lost."

Just before I panicked, Skeeter stepped up in front of Willie and said, "I ain't lost. I know my way 'round swamps. Y'all jes' follow me and stay right behind."

Off we went again, somehow confident of Skeeter's ability to get us out of this mess. Following along behind Skeeter and Willie, I thought about some Sunday lessons that we had at church. The lessons talked about how Moses had led the children of Israel out of Egypt through the desert across the Red Sea and into the promised land. Skeeter didn't look one bit like I thought Moses looked, but I sure prayed that he had some of Moses' skills when it came to being lost.

Willie had a brainstorm. "Look," he said. "Up through dem trees yonder. Dat's de power line dat runs through dis swamp and goes rat over de creek close to de grist mill."

I couldn't believe my ears. Willie had come through again. I was absolutely certain that Willie was the smartest boy my age in the whole world. I would petition my daddy soon as I got home to let me go to the Booker T. Washington School with Willie so I could be smart as him.

On we went. This time straight toward the power line that Willie had pointed out, with Skeeter still in front, Willie behind him, and me still in back. By now I was dragging the stringer, with the fish sliding along the ground behind me.

The sun was now getting down to where it was starting to fall behind the trees. We were just about to make our turn back eastward under the power line toward the big Talla-poosa Creek and the grist mill. Again, we were stopped. This time by Skeeter, who let out a yell loud enough to be heard back in town. "Holy damn shit!" he screamed. Me and Willie both were right up on his back looking over his shoulder toward the ground ahead of him. He was holding the little end of his cane pole on a snake so big that I couldn't tell where his tail ended.

"My God O'mighty!" were Skeeter's next words. "That's the biggest cottonmouth moccasin I've ever seen and I'm from Louisiana where biggun's are ever 'wher'. I'll hold down real hard on its head with the little end of my pole. Maybe I can hold him long enough for ya'll to fetch a limb to kill 'im with." But neither me nor Willie was going to leave the spot where we were standing to go off to look for a limb to kill that snake.

We kept watching that big cottonmouth moccasin. Our only comments were things like "Hold down real hard with yo' pole, maybe he'll die of exhaustion." I couldn't believe the size of the snake or the way it wrestled with all its might to get free of Skeeter's pole. Skeeter kept applying pressure to the back of the snake's head where the little end of his pole was placed. The snake was doing all kinds of wriggling and flopping, trying to get loose. Every time the snake lurched to one side or another, I could see its big broad snow-white belly. The top part of the snake was black, which made its white belly look whiter than it should. The snake had its mouth wide open, showing its long poisonous fangs. I stared hard at its mouth, realizing for the first time why that kind of snake is called a cottonmouth. Its big open mouth looked just like a large wad of cotton. We were all three about to die of fright. At least three times when a twig touched my leg, I thought that snake's partner had sneaked up behind me.

Skeeter continued his pleading. "If y'all don't get a big stick for me to kill this snake with, he'll 'ventually get loose and come right to us. You know cottonmouths are fighters.

25

They don't run from nothin'. Even a rattler will move out of yo way when it hears you comin', but a cottonmouth jes' ain't that way. They love a fight and will look you up to get one. We got to do something."

"That's right," I said. "We got to do something and I'm gonna pray for God to get us out of this snake predic'mint. I know in my heart that God sent this big ol' snake to punish us for all the bad words that's been said. Mostly by y'all, but some little bit by me too. God sent thangs to punish Job in the Bible, and He's now doing the same thing to us. Would y'all please join me in prayer?" I said as I began my plea to the Almighty.

"Lord," I spoke in my most reverent voice, "you know the sins of our hearts." Craaack! Skeeter's pole broke off about a foot from the snake's head. Skeeter was too much for that snake. Holding the majority of the cane pole left in his hand after the short piece broke off, Skeeter used the rest of the pole like a spear. He plunged the sharp small end right through that snake's head, pinning the snake, pole and all, to the ground.

"Foller, me" Skeeter yelled as we all lit out toward the creek and grist mill under the power line. We followed the clearing that was made by the power company to keep trees off their power line.

We were halfway to the grist mill, with me now out in front, taking long running strides. I remembered we had all left our poles, worm cans, and fish stringers back there with that snake. Never mind all that. By the time we reached the log footbridge, we were all running so hard that we nearly missed the log. We crossed back over the creek. Willie went his way back up the hill. Me and Skeeter continued back down the side of the creek to where I again took off for home. Skeeter made a beeline to his papa's trailer.

It was dark now and I knew this night's greetings for

26

me at home would be a lot worse than last night. Sure enough, Daddy, Momma, and Sister were waiting for me. This time from the edge of our front porch. Daddy was holding a big flashlight as if he was about to leave the house looking for me.

"Wash up and go to bed," was all that was said. When Daddy didn't say we would sit for a while, I knew I was in big trouble. Daddy never talked when he was mad. I went straight to bed, not looking forward to the next day.

FOUR

The best alarm clock for a growing boy is the smell of bacon frying in the pan. I was up and into my overalls in a flash, dashing through the kitchen on my way to the little wide spot between the kitchen and the dining room that Momma called the breakfast nook. Sister Evelyn came alongside me and asked if I had found the biscuit that she had left on my pillow last night.

What a shock! My sister really cared for my well-being, even enough to plant a leftover biscuit. She knew I'd be late and would have to go to bed without supper. That act of kindness may have changed my attitude toward my sister forever.

I had to admit to myself how shocked I had been to find that biscuit on my pillow last night. I was confused by its presence. Knowing how mad Daddy and Momma had been at my tardiness and never once thinking my sister might have done such, I reckoned it was sent by God like he did with the lost children of Israel when he sent the manna from heaven. Either that or the tooth fairy.

Now for the real thing, Momma's best breakfast. The blessing was pronounced by Daddy. The meal was quickly consumed as I was anxious to get started. I stood up to leave. "Not so fast," Daddy said. "It's time we talk." I sat back down, prepared for the worst. He continued, "It's Saturday and we must get some things done today. Tomorrow is Sunday and our first day at our new church home. After church, we've been invited to share a meal with Brother Otis

28

Kelly and his family. Besides being one of our deacons, Brother Kelly owns and operates the First National Bank. But first I want you," he said looking at me, "to take the lawn mower over all the front yard, then the back yard and then get all the weeds out of the shrubbery." It seemed like a month's work to me, but I didn't say a thing.

In a sterner voice than I had heard in years, Daddy continued, "What happened yesterday? You were gone from early morning till after dark. You had us all real worried. Tell us what happened."

I was ready. Dying to enlighten my family as to my recently discovered abilities as a goodwill ambassador, explorer, and fisherman, in rapid succession, I gave them a full accounting of my previous day's activities.

"Went straight from here down the street to the creek. Met Skeeter at the creek. We went up the creek to the old grist mill. Met up with Willie 'fore we got plum to the grist mill. Willie's a colored feller little older and little taller 'n me. Crossed the creek on a log footbridge. Went up the creek a little ways 'cause Willie was taking us to Devil's Slue. Found a good hole in Devil's Slue and caught gobs o' fish. Got lost! Runned up on a cottonmouth snake longer 'n me. Skeeter kilt the snake with his pole. Willie got us out under the power lines, and we got home just fine. I swear I believe ol' Willie's jes' like Moses."

When I finished my spiel, I looked at the three of them. They were looking back in total silence. They had the kind of stares that told me they were not as impressed as I thought they'd be.

Sister looked disgusted as usual. Momma seemed more worried than I could remember. Daddy had an expression that one might expect from a person with bad hemorrhoids. The silence was finally broken when Daddy said, "Get to work. There's much to be done, and we'll discuss this again later."

Fishin's a lot more fun than working. I figured that out. Big drops of sweat ran off my face, down my back, and tickled my back and belly on their way down. Back and forth across the yard.

"Watch out for the flowers. Don't dare cut into them," Momma said through the screen door. Back and forth I went. I was trying to get as much as I could with every pass while looking for something interesting to divert my attention. The something interesting came in the form of a big green lizard, maybe ten inches long. The lizard appeared out of nowhere in the uncut grass near the middle of the yard.

The lizard made a mad dash toward the front porch, trying to get under the house. I was pushing the lawn mower as fast as I could right behind him. I was too fast for that fat old green lizard. I ran right up him, and he went right through the lawn mower. I was left with two neat lizard halves in the freshly cut swath of grass behind the mower. Time out! It was time for me to examine my surgical prowess in the grass behind the mower. At first, I tried placing the lizard's mouth against the end of his tail. I then worked other combinations to see what effects I could gain. I was distracted by the shadow that appeared on the ground over me and the lizard. Looking up I found my daddy looking down at me and what I was doing. I remembered how Daddy was always opposed to the useless killing of anything. Quickly gathering my thoughts, I tried to put on the same look I remembered my daddy having at Aunt Sarah's funeral. I said, "I was mowing real fast when this pore ol' lizard here come a-runnin' straight at me and 'fore I knowed it, he runned right through this mower and passed on to paradise."

That clean-cut swath at an angle from the front toward the porch through all the uncut grass took a lot of sympathy out of the case that I was making. Daddy just walked on into the house.

With my bare foot, I kicked the lizard's remains on up under the porch. I gained some satisfaction out of getting that poor creature to the spot where he was headed at the time of his unfortunate accident.

By the time I had finished all the work I had been assigned by Daddy, it was almost as late as it was when I got home from yesterday's fishing trip. Sleeping was easy.

Getting ready for Sunday school and church is another of life's aggravations that needs elimination. I had gotten a blue suit for Christmas. It was already too little for me when I wore it at Easter. Now Momma said to wear it today. Since I don't have another suit, my choices were limited. My shoes are brown and too tight on my feet. The white socks make them feel tighter. Finally, my pants are on and after sucking in my stomach, they are buttoned. They need three more inches to reach my shoes. God forbid, Momma makes me put a little snap-on necktie into the collar of my only short-sleeved white shirt. It darn near choked me to death when Momma got it buttoned. With my suit coat finally in place, I examined myself in Momma's big mirror. I observed a distinct resemblance to many of the scarecrows that I saw in gardens on our way up from Shady Grove.

My pants felt especially tight in the straddle. I felt obliged to warn the family, "Sumpin' awful's gonna happen to me if I have to stoop over."

Sunday school and church were the same as they had been in Shady Grove. I can't remember much of Daddy's sermon. I do remember that part about how glad we were to be in this fine town and this congregation. I thought that part about being in this town was sure right for me because of Skeeter, Willie, and the fishin' holes.

When all the handshaking after church was over, we lit out, walking to Deacon Kelly's house. His house was a few blocks farther east toward the river and a few blocks to the north along a street with the biggest oak trees I ever saw.

Daddy and Momma walked in front, with me and sister Evelyn following close behind. The condition of my tight suit and the necktie was making me most uncomfortable. I inquired of Daddy as to why we didn't have a car or truck like some people in the church. Daddy allowed as to how "Preachers can't afford such things. Besides, everybody we need to see lives close enough for us to walk," he said. I told Daddy when I got grown I was gonna get rich off fishing and have three or four cars and trucks.

Mr. Kelly met us at his front door that opened up on the front porch of his big white house. Mr. Kelly was a dignified-looking man. He had on a business suit, with a buttoned vest. He was bigger and older than Daddy and wore big glasses that were black around the edges. He struck me as a feller completely in charge of everything around him. He led us into his living room next to the front door to meet his family. "Meet my wife, Gracie," he said. She smiled, stuck out her hand to Momma and Daddy, and then introduced her "darlin' children."

"This is my precious son, Dwight," she began. "He's eleven this month and will be in the sixth grade this year. He makes the best grades in his class." Mr. Kelly had to add his two cents worth about their shiny-faced boy, whom I already didn't like. He said, "Not only that, he cleans up the bank every day, takes out the trash, and does errands, like going to the post office for me." I thought for a minute that they might mention the wings he must be growing.

Mrs. Kelly was a heavy-set woman, with light colored

hair wound up in a neat ball on the back of her head. She wore small round glasses and had rings on both of her hands. One of her rings was a big shiny stone that made lights streak across the ceiling when she moved her hand a certain way, reflecting the sun coming through the window. She started introducing her two little girls. They were standing behind a small glass top table. "Meet my two darlin' twins," she said. I was looking straight at them and I thought I was seeing double. "They are six years old," said Mrs. Kelly. "Only three minutes apart, and they'll be starting school this September."

I couldn't believe my eyes. I was looking square in the face of the two ugliest human beings that I had ever seen. Had I not known better, I would have sworn they were two identical monkeys. They were dressed up in little matching green dresses, with square chunks of white lace around the parts of their dresses where their necks stuck through.

"We named our twins Adell and Artie Bell," said Mrs. Kelly, proud as a peacock. I could hardly keep from breaking out laughing. Why on Earth would their momma pick such an ugly name, as if to add insult to injury? With their fat round faces and eyes that seemed too close to their noses, they made me think about a neighbor's dog back at Shady Grove. The dog was called a Pick-a-Neese or something like that. Anyhow, I figured maybe Mrs. Kelly must have wanted their names to rhyme, but it did somehow make sense for the ugly girls to have ugly names. Those two little girls could scare a hungry dog off a meat wagon.

Throughout a sumptuous meal of fried chicken and all kinds of vegetables, Mrs. Kelly left nobody else a chance to say a word. She insisted on telling us more about her children. She got my attention real good when she started telling about her son Dwight. He was about the same size as me. His skin was way too pale for any boy. I figured he had to walk under a parasol when he went outside. The way his momma told it, I figured this boy must have never had one day of fun in his life. Among all his other achievements, he was now taking piano lessons. He would join other children in a piano recital in the library of the school one night next month. Recitals, I found out, was where children took turns playing little piano ditties. Their parents suffered through it, sitting in fold-out chairs, trying to look interested and proud.

Momma finally got a word in edgewise and said something about how she'd like to see me get interested in playing the piano like my sister. Evelyn had been playing the piano for three or four years. She even went so far as to say how if I did that, I could go play at a recital like Dwight. *Fat chance*, I thought. *I can't stand being cooped up over something dumb as a piano. Besides,* I thought, *my goin' to a recital would be like a hog goin' to a beauty parlor.*

Finally, it was good-bye time and I was much relieved. Going back to our house, I stayed way out in front of Daddy, Momma, and Evelyn. I was walking as fast as I could in my tight britches. I worried that one wrong move might result in serious harm to my lower body.

FIVE

A week is a mighty long spell of time when it's summertime in Alabama. It was pretty near a week now since I'd done anything 'cept just what Momma said to do. I'd washed more windows, trimmed more shrubs, and swept off more porches in less than one week than most folks do in a lifetime. Seemed like every time the breeze changed direction, Momma hollered for me to "Get the broom and sweep the porch." I just said "Yes'm" and did it. I needed to get back on her good side after that gettin' lost fishin' trip. 'Sides that, a boy ought'n never argue with his momma since you can't win anyway and it winds up changin' your plans.

I reminded Momma of my many accomplishments during my close to a week of enslavement. She acceded to my desire for a little time to walk down to where all the house trailers were parked in hopes of finding Skeeter.

As soon as Momma had finished lecturing me about the importance of being responsible regarding the feelings of other members of our family, I was off toward the trailer park, feeling free as a bird. I wasn't quite halfway to where the trailers were parked when I got near Mr. Taylor's General Mercantile Store. I spotted Skeeter sitting on a nail keg where the old men usually sat. The keg that he was on was one of three always left on the sidewalk under the porch of Mr. Taylor's store. Our meeting was a lot like going to a family reunion. Skeeter asked about what I'd been doing. He told me about him and his pa doing some fishing of their own.

Skeeter continued telling about everything him and his pa had done since I last saw him. Then Willie come around the corner of Mr. Taylor's store. Skeeter kept saying how he was gonna be just like his pa in every way, including that part about tearing out alligator jaws with his own bare hands the way his pa used to do in Louisiana. We welcomed Willie into our presence.

"What'ja been doin'?" Skeeter said to Willie.

"Heppin' Uncle Winslow at de grist mill," was Willie's reply.

Skeeter explained how him and Willie met here at Mr. Taylor's store " 'bout ever day this time." I was thinking how close we had been during my confinement of the last few days.

We made our way toward the door of Mr. Taylor's store to "look around and smell the goodies in the candy section." I spotted what appeared to be a shiny new penny lying in a crack of the plank floor of the sidewalk in front of the door. I moved toward the penny, now recognized by Willie. I heard him say, "Don't touch dat penny till you see if'n it's heads or tails. Never pick up a lost penny on tails 'less you ready for bad luck." The penny in question was showing its head in the up position. I grabbed it and we went inside the store. In a minute or so with our three noses against the glass protecting the candy, Skeeter asked, "How much is the Baby Ruth bar?"

"Ten cents," shot back Mr. Taylor.

Skeeter had a nickel, Willie had four cents, and my lucky penny made a dime. "See, I told you heads was lucky," said Willie. He had the grin of one with great wisdom. Skeeter took charge of the distribution of the candy bar. Using the end of his thumb from the knuckle out to the end of its fingernail for a ruler, he went to some length to divide the candy bar in three equal parts. Then he handed one piece to me, one to Willie, and kept one for himself. As we were about to devour the object of our delight, Mr. Taylor said, "Stop right there." We stopped and listened to Mr. Taylor's every word.

"The one who divides takes the smallest portion," said Mr. Taylor. He went on to explain that "Any man worth his salt when placed in the position of being the divider of any gain should always take the smaller portion for himself."

We stared at our chunks of the candy bar. Skeeter's chunk did look a tad bigger than ours. Skeeter swapped with Willie, mumbling something like, "Next time we git in this situation, somebody else can do the dividin'." We started dining on that wonderful Baby Ruth candy bar. We took little bites like a mouse might take, savoring each piece the way a wine taster might taste each sip.

Mr. Taylor was one of the nicest people I'd met since we moved here. I sure did like his old store. He said his store was one of the oldest around. "Made it through the Depression and World War Two without ever havin' to close 'er up," he often bragged. Mr. Taylor was a short, squatty man with a little bit of hair left. What's left was gray and he had a habit of rubbing his hand over his mostly bald head when he talked.

Wide wooden boards and a tin roof were used to construct Taylor's General Mercantile Store many years ago. Inside the store was found most anything a man might need. There were all kinds of plows, farm tools, and animal feed in the back. Work boots, bib overalls, and heavy duty work shirts were stacked on shelves along both sides.

In the middle of the store, near the back, Mr. Taylor kept large stacks of bags filled with seeds and fertilizer. In between the stacks of bags sat glass jars that contained a liquid the color of the water in big Tallapoosa Creek. Mr. Taylor said the jars were filled with a weed killer that he had developed himself. He said everybody who'd used his weed killer said it was the best they ever bought.

The front of the store was my favorite spot. That was where Mr. Taylor kept the candy, cold drinks, and fishing supplies.

Two old men parked their truck in front of the store and came inside. They started talking to Mr. Taylor about some of his weed killer that they had heard about. Before we left the store, the two men talking to Mr. Taylor said something about a Ku Klux Klan rally that was gonna be "round here somewhere soon." They also said a Grand Wizard was going to be there to make a speech. They said maybe as many as two hundred men and boys would probably show up.

My immense curiosity was working again! The word "rally" to me ranked almost as high as fishing hole. Besides, I had never seen a wizard of any kind. It sure sounded like a sight that I should see.

I hung around Mr. Taylor's store for a little while longer. During that time Skeeter explained how him and Willie met here every day when possible to "lay out their plans." I asked if we'd meet again tomorrow. Willie said he couldn't meet us tomorrow because he'd be helping his Uncle Winslow at the grist mill. He said we could come on up there if we liked.

We agreed on our next meeting at the grist mill tomorrow morning and left in our separate directions.

After supper, Momma and Sister were banging on the piano. Me and Daddy took our usual respite on the back porch. We listened to what Daddy called "God's natural choir of crickets and frogs." Daddy explained that the crickets made their noise by rubbing their legs together. The frogs made sounds by blowing air through little bags on their throats. He said they both did that to attract mates. I thought it would make a lot more sense if they just waltzed right up to a mate, stopped all that racket, and did whatever it was they were hollering about. Besides that, all that leg-rubbing must work a real sore on the crickets' legs, kind of like the way my tight britches almost did on Sunday.

Daddy was about ready to listen to me instead of the crickets and frogs. I didn't want to risk Momma and Sister joining us and thereby having the ignorance of my questions demonstrated to them, so I forged ahead with my question. I asked Daddy, "What's a Ku Klux Klan and a Grand Wizard?"

I knew I had asked an important question by the length of time Daddy took to stare out into nowhere and think about his answer before he started. When he finally did begin to talk, I felt as proud as Skeeter had said he felt when his pa talked to him the way that grown men speak to each other.

His words came slow and I hung on carefully to each. "The Ku Klux Klan is a large group of men and some nearly grown boys. No women, I'm told. They can be found 'most everywhere, but especially here in the Southern states. You don't hear too much about them till they get upset about things that you and I might not even notice. Then they gather up in big droves where they erect large crosses like what was used to crucify our Lord. They set fire to the cross. Then while the cross burns, they make loud speeches about one thing or another that bothers them. They are usually jumping around gettin' madder and madder. All the time they're doing their meetings they wear white sheets over their clothes. They call them robes and they wear white pointy-topped hoods over their heads. These have holes cut out for their eyes, nose, and mouth. The Grand Wizard is their leader, and he usually gets the maddest of all and has the most to say."

"What's they so all fired mad about?" I asked. Daddy

continued, "That's not so easy to say. It seems to me they are most likely people who enjoy getting mad in the first place. Beyond that, I don't know much more about them since I've never knowingly talked to one. I probably have without knowing. I can say from what I have heard that they seem to be the kind of folks who look for some other person on whom to lay blame for their own misery and misfortune. I can tell you for sure that you're better off never mentioning those people. Just go about your life like they don't exist and never go near their premises."

"Yessir," I said feeling more curiosity than ever. Robes, hoods, burning crosses, and Grand Wizards had the makings of a great adventure.

Daddy stayed busy as a bee every day from early morning till dusk dark, "canvassing the town," as he called it. Sometimes he took me with him. I found out that "canvassing the town" meant walking to every building in the entire town. At each place he would introduce himself and talk to them about God and coming to church.

Sometimes when I was with him, we'd find people at home and set on their porch with them. If they had a porch. One day we came up to a little "straight-through" house that folks called a shotgun house. An old man was sitting by himself on the front porch. The old man invited me and Daddy to come up on his porch and visit with him "for a spell." When we set down in the chairs next to the old man, I spotted a bucket of water on a small table next to him. The bucket had a dipper for drinking the water. The old man musta been dippin' snuff or had chewin' tobacco in his mouth. He kept spittin' out over the edge of the porch into the yard, leavin' little dribbles across the boards of his porch. He had some front teeth that had rotted, which 'caused some of the tobacco juice to gather on his chin on both sides of his mouth.

While Daddy was tellin' the old man 'bout us, the church, and how God loved him, I got real thirsty. I asked the old man if I could use his dipper and get me a drink of water from his water bucket. He said, "He'p yo'seff, youn-gun'," which I did while catching Daddy's look that told me he'd wished I hadn't asked for the water.

I used the dipper and drank enough water to satisfy my thirst. I thanked the old man for his water. He answered in a way that me and Daddy could tell he was happy to have something to share with us. I knowed Daddy must have been real thirsty too and couldn't understand why he didn't grab that dipper and do as I'd done, especially since the old man seemed to enjoy sharin' his water. I could tell Daddy didn't want to drink from the old man's dipper. He was probably scared off by the looks of the old man's teeth and the tobacco juice on his chin.

The old man looked at Daddy in a way that said he thought Daddy was feeling too high-fallutin' for his water. Daddy decided he was also thirsty and reached for the dipper.

Me and the old man watched as Daddy carefully lifted a dipper of water from the bucket. Daddy brought the dipper up to his mouth and then eased the dipper handle up next to his ear. Holding the dipper handle next to his ear, Daddy put his mouth on the dipper at the spot right next to where the handle ends on the dipper. At that point Daddy tilted the dipper up carefully to his mouth. When Daddy finished drinking the water in the dipper, he carefully replaced the dipper in the bucket. When he turned to sit back down, the old man looked at Daddy with a great big smile of satisfaction and said, "Well, darn, Preacher, I'm sure glad I got to meet you. You're the only other feller that drinks water from a dipper at the same place on the dipper that I do." Daddy got pale and seemed like he was chokin'.

SIX

Grist mill, here I come! I explained to Daddy how important it was to my education to learn about grist mills. He allowed my departure with my promise to be back early to help with some chores before nightfall.

Hot sun, bare feet, things to learn, and people to meet. That was all that was required to assure a short trip from my house to the grist mill.

When I arrived at the grist mill, which was an old wooden building perched out over the edge of the water in the mill pond, I went straight through the open door and found Willie sitting on the floor in front of a large pile of dry ears of corn. Willie was hard at work. He would pick up one of the ears of dry corn piled on the floor, put his fingers into the top end of the "leaves" of the ear of corn that Willie called "shucks," and pull the shucks back to the big end of the ear of corn. Then he broke them off, leaving a shiny big ear of yellow corn. It was zap, zap, zap and Willie was holding another ear of cleaned yellow corn.

A large black man stepped through the door. He was wearing faded blue overalls and a straw hat. I saw he had a head of snow-white hair when he took his hat off to use for a fan. "Who's dis boy here?" asked the old man.

"He's called Junior," said Willie. He went on to explain my presence in their town as the son of the new preacher at the First Baptist Church.

Then Willie introduced me to the old man with white hair. "Dis my Uncle Winslow," he said. He went on to say

42

how the old man was the brother of the grandma he lived with, which really made Mr. Winslow the uncle of his momma. That made the old man Willie's great-uncle. Anyhow, the old man smiled at me real big, stuck out his hand, and said, "Welcome, boy. You and Willie's done got to be friends, I see."

"Yessir, Mr. Winslow," I said, looking at my hand completely lost in his own halfway up my elbow. "I never been in no grist mill before. I sure would like to know how it works," I said to Mr. Winslow, whose smile got even bigger. He said, "You come to the right place."

Mr. Winslow took me over to the far side of the grist mill. There, a big handle hung down within reaching distance. The other end of the handle was attached to a wire rope. The rope extended down to a steel plate sitting inside two grooves carved into the sides of a small ditch. The ditch led from the water pond into a chute that ran out to the side of a giant water wheel.

Mr. Winslow went on to explain how he could pull down on the long handle that would lift the metal plate up from the small ditch below. That allowed the water through the chute over the giant wheel, which then set everything in motion.

He showed me a shaft running from the center of the giant wheel through the side of the bottom of the grist mill. That was attached to a smaller wheel on the dry side of the wheel embankment. The small wheel had a large belt wrapped around it that ran up to a wheel over the grind stone. When the water wheel moved round and round, the grind wheel inside the grist mill moved in circles against its base stone. The result was stone ground corn meal, which Mr. Winslow declared to be the world's best.

We walked over to a machine about half as tall as me that Mr. Winslow called a corn sheller. He took ears of shucked corn that were shucked by Willie and started putting them, "little end first," into the corn sheller. He then started turning the crank of the corn sheller, which sent the kernels of corn down into a large bucket under the machine. The long white and red cobs from which the corn kernels had been taken fell to the side. When the bucket below the sheller was full, Mr. Winslow took it over to the grinder. Then he poured it into what he called a hopper above the grinder. It looked to me like a bucket with a pointed bottom. He pulled a lever at the bottom of the hopper, which sent the corn rushing into the grinder. From there it emerged out the side of the grinder as fresh ground corn meal. The corn meal smelled good enough to eat coming out of the grinder. Mr. Winslow showed me how to run the sheller while he helped Willie with the shucking. He promised us both a good taste of the corn meal for our lunch.

When all the pile of corn I had found in front of Willie on my arrival had been shucked, shelled, and run through the grinder, Mr. Winslow said it was time to taste the same kind of corn meal we had been making. With that, he produced three tin plates from a wooden box next to the wall. They looked to me like the pans that Momma used to make pies. In each plate he poured a layer of syrup from a small tin bucket also stored in the wooden box. After that, he opened a large brown paper bag. From the bag he took a big round cake of cornbread. He said he cooked the cornbread before leaving his house this morning. From that I learned the simple joy of what Mr. Winslow called soppin'.

Soppin' ain't nothing more than holding one end of the bread with your fingers while stirring the other end around in the syrup until it's good and wet with syrup. Then you put it in your mouth and smile while you chew. After turning that sheller crank, I found cornbread and syrup far better than the ice cream that we had at church socials.

We sat on the floor of the grist mill, leaning our backs against the wall with the door and windows wide open. A gentle breeze came through and we discussed everything of interest to my mind.

Mr. Winslow talked about his concern for the sickness now being felt by his sister. That seemed to worry Willie, especially since that was the grandma with whom he lived.

Mr. Winslow talked at length about how he had once made a real good living from his grist mill. But that was before people started buying their corn meal at a store or making biscuits. He said some even bought bread cut up in slices and packaged for the stores by "God knows who." Anyhow, his best days with the grist mill were a long time ago. Now he had to rely on those few remaining folks who brought their corn to him so they could keep eating cornbread made the old-fashioned way.

Skeeter finally showed up too late for the cornbread and syrup. He said he didn't care since his pa had left him a whole quarter this morning and he had used the quarter to fill his stomach at Mr. Taylor's store before "drifting on up to check on y'all."

Skeeter sat down on the floor and leaned back against the wall like the rest of us. It got quiet again. Mr. Winslow's eyes were closed and that same question that was nagging me last night was doing it again.

As if speaking to everyone, but nobody in particular, I asked, "What's a Ku Klux Klan and a Grand Wizard?"

Mr. Winslow's eyes popped open. "Boy," he said "dat's a bunch you don't need to know nuttin' about. Dey ain't nuttin' but a gang of rabble-rousers, blamin' they problems on black folks."

That was my first inkling of the color of skin being a part of the problem. Maybe my daddy hadn't been totally honest with his answers last night. Maybe he'd been trying too hard to shelter me from problems around us in hopes of my developing "a mind and heart with malice toward no one." Regardless of who was at fault, the whole thing had my mind made up for good. I stepped outside where Skeeter and Willie had gone right after my question. I walked up to them, out of hearing range of Mr. Winslow who was cleaning up in the grist mill. I announced my intentions. "We're goin' to go to that Klan rally and see for ourselves what's they all about."

"You crazier 'n a bed bug," said Skeeter.

"No use you sayin' we," Willie declared. "Them folks would kilt me on the spot dey fount me and you, too, if'n yo daddy weren't a preacher."

That last remark stung me good. Especially that part about being the preacher's boy. I took off for home. Stopping briefly a few yards from where I left them standing, I hollered back real loud, "I double dog dare you to take me up on trying." Then to add a little insult, I yelled, "Anybody that'll take a dare will steal a goat and eat its hair." *That ought to do it*, I thought.

SEVEN

The days were getting longer and longer. The sun was getting hotter and hotter. All I did was sweep off the porches when Momma said sweep and push that mower over the yard when Daddy said mow. Sometimes I just sat and stared. I swear I was looking at the grass in the front yard yesterday and saw it growing right before my eyes.

One feller down at Mr. Taylor's store said there was going to be a picture show started up soon. Some folks from Birmingham was going round startin' picture shows in old store buildings no longer being used. There was two or three like that around here that could be used. The thought of getting a picture show in town sounded real good to me, and I hoped it came soon.

Another old man playing checkers at the store was telling the other old man playing with him about something he called television that was coming our way. "They already got it in Birmingham," he said, "and it won't be much longer till we'll have it here." I had asked him what television was, and he said it was "nothin' more'n a big radio with a glass front so you'll see everything goin' on in the radio." Just like a picture show, I figured. I'd seen picture shows when we lived in Shady Grove, bein's it's close to Birmingham. They was real fun to me. "Television'll be here soon as the wires get long enough to come from Birmingham plumb over Sand Mountain and down to where we live," the old man had concluded. *I hope it's soon,* I thought.

Going down to Mr. Taylor's store every day hoping to

find Skeeter and Willie was something to really look forward to. I found a tin can with both ends still in place. Its contents had been drained through two small holes punched in the top. I set the can down on the sidewalk in front of our house and begin kicking the can in the direction of the store. The first time it took twenty-nine kicks to get the can down to Mr. Taylor's store. I told Skeeter and Willie about my devising this game and how good I'd be at it by the time school started back. "I bet by then one kick will send this can from our house to the store," I boasted. That tin can seemed to shorten the days by just a little. I was soon down to twenty-three kicks from our house to the store. Then a truck loaded with potatoes coming in from a farm north of town flattened my can when one of my shorter kicks failed to get the can across the street. It ain't easy finding a tin can with both ends still left. Since kicking cans with one end cut out can cause cuts between the toes, I gave up can kicking. Life goes on.

Wasn't long though before I got to the store one morning early before the old men had started their checkers game. I found Willie and Skeeter looking hard at some writing on a piece of paper taped to the window of Mr. Taylor's store. I stuck my head up to the paper they were reading. It was plain to see a real live carnival was coming to town! This coming Saturday, all day and into the night. There'd be merry-go-rounds, a Ferris wheel, and things Willie said would "jerk ya guts out." There'd be cotton candy, homemade ice cream, and all sorts of games to play for a nickel or dime that gave prizes to winners.

Me and Willie and Skeeter talked about when we'd meet at the carnival place. The sign said it was to be in the little open pasture behind the school. I said, "Let's be there when it opens," but Willie said he couldn't 'cause of work to do. Skeeter couldn't either, so we said three o'clock at the gate.

Waitin' for that comin' Saturday was a lot like waitin' on Christmas when the tree's been decorated. Saturday finally got there. I fished five nickels from a fruit jar with a hole in the lid that I kept under my bed. I waited impatiently for three o'clock. I could already hear screams from the folks "gettin' their guts jerked out" long before I could leave to meet Willie and Skeeter at three o'clock.

I was at the entrance gate of the carnival before my companions arrived. I kept standing on first one foot then the other, looking both directions at the same time, wondering if they'd ever show up.

Finally they arrived and in we went, looking at everything at once. A nickel for the merry-go-round, a nickel for the Ferris wheel, a nickel to get our guts jerked out. Then over to the cotton candy machine, another nickel and I was 'bout outta money.

"Time to watch people play games for prizes," was Skeeter's suggestion. We went from game booth to game booth, watching them all. We came upon one booth in particular that got the attention of us all. There was this long chute kind of thing about thirty feet long with canvas walls. The walls were seven or eight feet apart. The canvas was pulled up high around the walls and taken across the top to the other wall, forming something that looked kind of like a tunnel. The tunnel led down to the far end to a little gray monkey 'bout three feet tall. The monkey was waving its arms and standing on its hind legs. A man in red suspenders was yelling his lungs out 'bout how fast the monkey was.

"Step right up, ladies and gentlemen, and see the quickest monkey in the entire world," said the man. "This monkey's been plumb 'round the world with me from Little Rock, Arkansas, to Waycross, Georgia, waving his arms and dodgin' tennis balls thrown at him. For one nickel you git three tennis balls to try to hit that monkey. If you even raise one hair on the monkey, you git this here giant stuffed Teddy bear. It's bigger'n the monkey hisself. Ain't been but one ole boy over'n Wiggins, Mississippi, ever touched that monkey with one o' them tennis balls. I know ain't nobody 'round here good as them boys in Wiggins."

That's all it took. Folks started getting in line. They handed over nickels, taking three tries each to hit that little monkey with a tennis ball. Whoosh, whoosh, whoosh—tennis balls were thrown at the monkey. Not a hair was touched on the monkey. He was quicker'n greased lightning. The monkey would even tease the throwers by letting the tennis ball get right at its head or stomach, then "whuff," he would move. The monkey felt only the breeze off the ball going past.

Fastballs, curveballs, knuckleballs, sinkerballs, and one ball bouncing off the canvas wall. That ball was an errant pitch of a woman who tested her pitching arm against the monkey. That was the only pitch that came close to hitting the monkey. He failed to watch the ball after it hit the wall and it almost got him on his foot.

Willie got in line, gave the man in charge his nickel, and took the three tennis balls. Willie put one ball in his pocket. Then he stepped up to the front of the monkey chute, holding one ball in his left hand and one in his right. Willie began moving his outstretched left arm up and down with the tennis ball very visible in the palm of his hand. The monkey's eyes locked into the rhythm of Willie's up and down motion of his left arm. Then Willie tossed the ball gently up in the air over the monkey's head. While the monkey watched the ball over its head, "whop" Willie got the monkey with the ball he'd been holding in his right hand.

"That's all for now, folks," said the man in charge of the

monkey. After that, he nailed a small sign to the top of the monkey chute. The sign said "only one ball at a time." I felt as proud as a member of a world champion team of some kind, walking around the carnival grounds next to Willie. He was holding his giant Teddy bear as if it was a trophy.

There was also a big ring set up not far from the monkey chute that looked like pictures I'd seen of a boxing ring. Lots of people were gathered round that ring that Skeeter said wuz a bear-wrestling ring. We watched the goin's on in the bear-wrestling ring for a few minutes. The feller in charge of the bear looked and sounded like the feller in charge of the monkey. He was hollerin' about how you could pay a dime to get in the ring with the bear. If you put the bear on his knees, you'd get a brand spankin' new five dollar bill.

Since Willie was the biggest, me 'n' Skeeter put in on him to get in the bear ring and wrestle the bear. We even said how we'd muster up the ten cents 'twixt us. Skeeter told how they wuz a famous football coach in Alabama that he'd heard about who got his name of "Bear" from wrestling a bear just like this one when he was a boy in Arkansas.

"Nope," was all Willie said, clutching his giant Teddy bear. "I got all de prize I need. I ain't turnin' it loose till I put it in my granny's hands. She'll love dis critter."

Willie did make one last comment before we left the bear ring. He stood up tall, as if to show us just how big he was. Then he said, "If'n I did get in dat ring wit dat bear, I'd sho 'nuff win, no doubt 'bout dat. I'd jes grab dat bear by his go-nads, squeeze real hard, and dat bear'd be on his knees beggin' 'fo' you'd say scat."

That made me even prouder of Willie, knowin' he could outsmart a bear and a monkey.

After we left the bear wrestling ring, we walked further around the carnival grounds. I spotted that same girl with the long blond hair who rode her bicycle in front of our house. She was standing in front of where they sold ice cream between a man and lady. I figured they were her parents. I could have sworn that she smiled at me and maybe even waved a little. I didn't say nothing, not wanting Willie and Skeeter to detect any interest on my part. I was thinking how I might go out and ride a bicycle along with her if I had a bicycle.

I had been after Santa Claus for the last three or four years about bringing me a bicycle. Last year I figured out who Santa Claus was and how he was too broke to bring me a bicycle.

We left the carnival grounds, vowing to meet up again soon, but not before I reminded them of my intentions to sneak into the Klan rally, if it ever happened.

EIGHT

Revivals are big events in Baptist churches. Especially so in Alabama. Most Baptist churches have two or three a year. There is always one in the summertime. At this time, air-conditioning hadn't made it to most Baptist churches in Alabama. The church meetings, even at night, became a little too warm for most except the very dedicated. Beads of sweat cooled gently by the steady waving of "funeral home fans" was something I grew accustomed to years ago. Funeral-home fans are square pieces of cardboard about one foot square. The squares are stapled to a small wooden handle with the name of the local mortuary printed in large letters on one side. A picture of something like the Last Supper is on the other side.

Preparation for revivals begins with excited remarks regarding the evangelist who'll be coming to lead the revival. He'll have some special talent for ciphering the Scriptures. Beginning a few weeks before the first day of revival, the pastor of the church holding the revival feels obliged to lay a considerable layer of guilt on his congregation. He always comes down real hard on how the church has been negligent about going into the "highways and byways" of the community to search out lost souls in need of salvation. Some Baptist preachers are so good at laying on guilt, it makes you want to bust right out in the middle of his sermon and start finding those lost souls. The First Baptist Church of Rainbow Junction was now in "the gettin' ready mode."

Revivals can be real good times if you get a revival preacher who knows when to quit. I swear, last year I thought I was gonna miss a birthday during one night of the summer revival. That preacher seemed determined to talk till somebody came up to the front to confess their sins, and nobody budged.

Revival time was here. Starting Monday night, seven o'clock sharp. Everybody seemed ready, wound up tighter'n an eight-day clock.

Daddy'd been praying his heart out with us every night. He asked God's will for our lives and His help in our search for sinners. Momma had lined up several ladies whom she will bring to the revival. Daddy had many on his list. Even Sister had three or four. I had none so far. I was beginning to get a powerful surge of guilt.

During our last back-porch session prior to the start of revival, Daddy asked if I had found any visitors to bring. Not wanting to look any less evangelistic than the rest of our family, I said, "Yessir, Skeeter 'n Willie."

One of Daddy's eyebrows raised up a little. Then he got a wrinkle across his face the way he always did when he's worried. He thought for a minute, then started speaking. "Son," he said, "you have gradually been taking me in a direction I've been trying to avoid. You see, I'm fearful of winding up being the one to address a sensitive subject that could result in your misunderstanding my point. Saying just one word on that subject that you might not fully understand could lead to my having become a party to the tainting of the wholesome attitude you now have for all people."

Hearing that, I was proud but a little confused at the same time. "You see," he said, "I derive great pleasure from my observation of your relationships with people you meet. I take great pride in your openness and honesty with everyone. I feel that God has answered my prayer by giving you

54

the people qualities you have. I've dreaded the day when those qualities would be tested by some social customs of our society."

I liked what he's saying, I think. He went further. "Here in the South there's a custom about white folks going to white church congregations and colored folks going to church with colored congregations. I hope you understand. I pray what I've told you won't change your outlook on life."

"But what if Willie preferred our church? And what if God turns out to be black? You always said nobody knowed what color he was. Sister said God might even be a woman. Wouldn't that be somethin'. We'd all sweep porches for eternity!"

Daddy sat there and heard all my arguments. Then, like a kindly old judge, he said, "I hear what you're saying and see the merit in every word, but for now don't pull on Willie. Don't change your outlook, just wait in peace. Someday all of this will change."

We had it settled. I would lay off Willie. I could go after Skeeter. Things would change. In my mind that meant in time for the next revival.

The revival got started and the singing was wonderful. There's something about standing between those church pews with all those songs being sung that sends a real sweet-like feeling deep down into my soul. I can't say exactly what that feeling is, but I can say after I felt it, lying didn't come near as easy.

The revival was in full swing. People were being brought in from all directions. The visiting evangelist was in top form. The funeral home fans were working overtime. Everybody was bringing people to the church except me, so I bore down on Skeeter.

"Heck, no!" was Skeeter's first reply to my request for

his presence in our church congregation. "Last time I went to church was with my pa three or four years ago. We wuz back in Louisiana." He said a priest got up and said somethin' in a foreign language, but he didn't see much to it. I tried to explain the possibilities to be derived from going to our revival. I told him he could be winding up in a place with pearly gates and streets of gold. Skeeter didn't seem impressed. We continued for a while, sharing the bench under a tree in front of the door to their little trailer.

I switched tactics, figuring I might scare him into going with me. "If'n you don't never go to church, the Devil's gonna gitcha," I implored. "Ain't nothin' gittin' me long as Pa's round," Skeeter replied. I switched tactics again. "Look, Daddy bought me six new fish hooks and two big red bobbers. I'll split'em if you go," I said, feeling much guilt for resorting to bribery. "Nope!" was all he said.

I was nowhere near ready to give up. Skeeter was my only chance of avoiding a shutout in the game of getting visitors to church. I raised my voice a little and said with some aggression, "Okay, Mr. Big Shot, what you got against our church?" I thought that putting him on defense might yield better results. Bing! I hit the right button.

"It's that sissy-ass Dwight Kelly," he said. "He goes to that church and I knows him good from school. He's always walking 'round in his fancy duds with his nose turned up so high he would drowned if he's caught out in a heavy rain. He's always struttin' round school, braggin' on hisself and makin' fun o' me. I tell you for sure, I'm gonna bloody his nose good when I catch him out o' sight of the teacher." Skeeter's hostility surprised me, but at least he didn't say no. I felt I had him leaning my way.

"Look," I said, as I moved in on my first opportunity to close this negotiation. "Dwight don't go every night and

56

even if he was there, we'd just sashay right past him and go to the front row. That's where Daddy likes me to sit."

Finally, Skeeter relented. "Okay, if it'll stop your whining. After Pa gets here, I'll eat and go with you, but I promise I'll bloody that sissy boy's nose if I catch him outside."

"No problem," I said, ready to make any compromise to get me off the hook. "I'll wait with you." I'd told Momma before I left the house that I might just have to meet her at church if things didn't go right. She had said O.K., but she added that "if things didn't go right" meant even one fish hook of mine in the water, she'd have Daddy apply some "rod of correction" after church.

Skeeter's pa showed up just before church time and allowed me to share their sardines taken straight from a flat tin box. He also brought saltine crackers that he picked up at the store on his way home. We ate off the table next to the bench that we'd been occupying. Having peeked at the inside of their trailer and enjoying a "man's meal" outside, I didn't feel near as much sympathy for Skeeter not having a momma. His kind of living struck me as being perfect.

Looking at Skeeter's pa, I understood Skeeter's lack of fear for his safety. That was the biggest man I'd ever seen. He was not fat, just big. He had on a T-shirt and his arms looked to me as big as tree limbs of an oak tree. He looked like the kind of man who would go bear hunting with a broomstick. He had the same kind of dark hair as Skeeter. He was real dark brown from all the sunshine that he got from working outside. He didn't talk much, but when he did, I noticed he spoke more like one of us. Listening to him and Skeeter, I got the feeling they were more like buddies than father and son.

I was enjoying the meal with Skeeter and his pa so much that I almost forgot church. I realized we might be late, so I said good-bye to Skeeter's pa, grabbed Skeeter, and ran.

By the time we got inside the front door of the church, everybody was on their feet. They were all standing up with their heads bowed as the visiting evangelist opened the service with prayer. I was grateful for our timing, thinking we would have plenty of time to get down to the front row before the prayer was over. I intended to be seated before Daddy straightened up to look my way.

Before we took our first step forward, Skeeter pointed and I looked. There was Dwight Kelly standing pretty as you please next to his momma. They were in the second row from the back. Not only that, he was standing at the end of the pew next to the aisle that we were headed down. That's where his daddy always stood. I supposed Dwight's daddy had some good reason not to attend tonight's service, so Dwight got to stand at his daddy's spot with his momma right beside him. Dwight would be only inches away from us as we moved past. I was sure Skeeter wouldn't dare hit anybody in church, so I pulled on the sleeve of his shirt and started walking.

As I passed the end of the pew where Dwight Kelly stood, I realized Skeeter had stopped. I turned around to see what he was doing. In a brief minute that seemed like an hour, I stood horrified. Skeeter extended his right arm out in Dwight's direction. He then folded four fingers into his hand, leaving his middle index finger sticking up toward Dwight. He tried to shield the gesture from people in the choir with his left hand.

I was very grateful that nobody but Dwight could see what happened. His momma might have since she fell back on her pew, fanning as fast as she could like she had a bad case o' vapors.

I pulled hard on Skeeter and we made it to the front

pew before the prayer was finished. Daddy raised his head at the end of the prayer, looked at me, and smiled.

I didn't get much from that church service. I was thinking too much about Skeeter. First I was mad at him for the evil thing he did, especially in church. Then I felt sympathy for his not having a momma and all. I even remembered what one old man at Mr. Taylor's store had said about Skeeter. "That boy ain't got no do-right in 'im." I still felt proud of having brought one visitor. I figured next time I'd have two 'cause by then me 'n' God would have things worked out so that Willie would be welcomed.

NINE

Deacon Johnson came by last night. Momma met him at our front door, then she brought him to the back porch where me and Daddy was sittin'. The deacon said he had church business to discuss, so Daddy told me to go to bed. I did, but my bedroom had a window that opened to the far end of the back porch. That was close to the end where they were sitting. Long as I didn't get in bed and kept my ear next to the window, I could hear mostly every word they said.

Deacon Johnson began his talking to Daddy in a more solemn voice than he had when we first looked at the town from the top of Sand Mountain. "That was a fine revival we had last week and your own sermons have blessed us all. Your lovely wife and daughter have already provided some much needed help with our Sunday school program, for which we're all very grateful." I noticed he hadn't got around to me yet. I was gettin' a little nervous.

"Some of the men in church have asked me to speak to you about your boy. Now, he ain't real bad, mind you. He ain't probably no worse than I was as a boy. But being the pastor's son and all . . . (pause) . . . well, you know what I mean. Folks always thinks the preacher's boy has to be better'n other boys so's to set a good example. Now don't get me wrong. I don't see nothin' much to what they say, but being I was the chairman of the committee that found you and I was the first to meet y'all and everything, the other men thought maybe I ought to be the one to bring all this up to you. But again, not meaning to say anything ugly and think-

60

ing maybe it is 'cause our church ain't never had a preacher with a boy in my lifetime—they was all blessed with girls—so maybe it's just like we don't know exactly what a preacher's boy ought to be like."

"Could you be a little more specific, Brother Johnson?" Daddy asked.

"Well," Mr. Johnson began, "it's common knowledge, since y'all got here your boy Junior spends his spare time cavortin' with colored folks and others of dubious character."

Daddy answered in a most proper tone. "Brother Johnson," he began, "Junior is a fine boy and I'm glad you recognize that. Junior and I have recently discussed a small portion of this subject. I feel certain his actions are not intended to reflect poorly on our church in any way. I'll continue to discuss this subject with Junior but never in a way that might encourage him to forsake his open-minded love and respect for all people."

"That's fine," said Mr. Johnson as he got up to leave. "But remember, little things like we've talked about here has ways of getting blown up so big in little country churches like ours to the point of making things difficult for everybody."

"I understand," Daddy said, "and I'll keep what you've said in mind. Good night, Brother Johnson."

"Good night, Preacher."

I went to bed fast, closed my eyes, and thought real hard. *How do I find out what "cavortin' " and "dubious" was without asking Daddy so he'd find out I'd been eavesdropping?*

I don't think Daddy said anything to anybody about his conversation with Deacon Johnson. Anyhow, I started back cavortin' the next day with Willie and Skeeter.

No sooner had I got to the front of the store, when I heard the news. The Ku Klux Klan rally was for certain now comin' in no more than a week or two at the most. The Klan don't post signs announcing their meeting's time nor place. They don't like uninvited guests. They let their people know with secret code words and handshakes, according to Mr. Taylor.

I told Skeeter and Willie, "I sure wish I could get my hands on their secret code words and handshakes. Then I'd just march right into their rally and scour round till I knowed all they was to know 'bout Klannin'."

Willie and Skeeter both said that codes and handshakes wouldn't help us none. If we went to that rally without being invited by one of them, we'd likely be strung up.

I wouldn't accept no for an answer. I explained how we could approach their gate, make some distraction, and slip right by when they looked the other way.

Willie said, "You got 'bout as much chance slippin' by dem people as you'd have slippin' daylight past a rooster." That did not slow my interest in "completing our plans for a field trip to a Klan rally," as I preferred to call my proposal. "Total fool you are," Skeeter snorted. "Amen," said Willie. "Don't know when it's comin' or where it'll be," I said, "but I plan for us to join them somehow, someway."

When I got back to our house, I went to the kitchen to check out any leftovers and found Sister Evelyn sitting pouty-faced at the table. "What's wrong with you?" I asked. "I swear you're sittin' there all pouted up lookin' like somebody done licked all the red off your stick of candy."

"You know what's wrong," she said. "Everybody in town's been talking 'bout you. They're saying you ain't fit to be a preacher's boy. You better suited to be somebody called Huckleberry Finn."

"Huh," I grunted. "Bet I know more 'bout fishin' 'n that Huckleberry feller."

Sister went on jabberin' for a while about my actions

since getting to our new home. She said I was causing her considerable embarrassment and grief.

I allowed as to how I wasn't doing nothing more than what felt natural. I reminded her how I had gone out much like a missionary and found Skeeter. I got him to church for a revival meeting, which was a whole lot more'n most people would do.

Sister made a real sour face at the mention of Skeeter's name. That made me start thinking of his unkindly gesture toward Dwight on our way into church. Maybe it had leaked out.

Gettin' in the last word in our little debate, I reminded Sister what Daddy always said. To go through life "doing what's right and enjoying what you do." I figured that fit me perfectly and dropped it there.

Being a member of a preacher's family means everything in life revolves around the church. Sunday school on Sunday morning, followed by a preaching service. Bible training on Sunday night, followed by a preaching service. Prayer meetings and choir practice every Wednesday night. Revivals, visitations, and social gatherings of every imaginable sort are thrown in for good measure. Most folks I knew seemed to have developed some sort of immunity to the effects of all this activity. They simply participated without raising questions. I was not so lucky. I seemed to be hung up on questions about a lot of our doin's that didn't get answered unless I asked.

Like last Sunday during Sunday school. The subject was heaven, which generally shares equal billing with hell at Baptist churches. Just like many times before, the teacher was saying how heaven had pearly gates and streets of gold and everybody sprouted wings to help them get about. Since I didn't see much use in gates of pearl and the gold on the street didn't seem important to me, I asked for more detail. I flat out stated my concern for the wings gettin' in the way of puttin' on my shirt. The teacher said there was more to it than that.

"Heaven," the teacher said, "is all of the best things in life that your mind is capable of imagining. If you really must know what heaven will be like, just recite the ten most wonderful things your mind can conceive and multiply by thousands."

I couldn't yet multiply by thousands, but I could quickly reel off the ten best things, which I proceeded to do without being asked. "Fishin' holes, fishin' hooks, wiggle worms, candy bars, cornbread soppin'—"

"Thank you, we understand," the teacher interrupted. "That's fine, Junior. We got your message and we'll come back to that one day."

I wasn't sure I know anymore of what heaven was like and I wasn't sure the teacher did either. I was sure that I wasn't gonna be satisfied till I found out.

The more questions I got worked out in my head, the more seemed to fill in. Daddy said King Solomon was the wisest mortal man ever to walk the Earth. Daddy also said King Solomon answered so many important questions for hisself till it just about drove him crazy. Daddy read me what King Solomon wrote in his book called Ecclesiastes at the very end of the first chapter. The king said he increased his knowledge, which increased his grief. Then right behind that he said he increased his wisdom, which increased his sorrow. I felt bad for King Solomon, but I couldn't stop questions from comin' to my mind.

TEN

The sun comes up 'fore anybody's ready in the summertime. The minute the sun popped up, the breeze through my window stopped. When that happened it was hard to stay in the house for very long.

Besides, I liked gettin' started early, especially when there ain't nothing that had to be done. If I grabbed a biscuit and went before Momma remembered the porch needed sweeping, my day got off to a better start.

Down the street toward the store was the Huggins house. Their house wouldn't be no different than all the other houses if it weren't for the giant honeysuckle vine. That vine covered their fence all the way to the corner. It was loaded with white and yellow flowers thick as hair on a dog's back. The flowers now had enough summertime behind them to make them give off a most delicious odor. I stopped right beside the honeysuckle vine and took deep breaths through my nose. I let that good smell drift through my nostrils and filter all the way into every corner of my body. Honeysuckle is to smelling what church hymns is to feeling good. They both do things for your soul.

Wasn't nobody at the store except Mr. Taylor and two old men leaning up on his counter top. They were talking about the Klan rally and how they was worried 'bout all the trouble brewing in Birmingham by black folks. They said how they wished the Klan would find some other town for their rally. "Folks 'round here don't need that stuff."

Having no further interest in the conversations at the

store, I took off for the grist mill, hoping to find my companions.

I took the dirt road that ran behind the store over to the creek and up to the grist mill. That allowed me to arrive at my second best meeting spot in a matter of minutes.

Getting within seeing distance of the grist mill, I spotted Mr. Winslow sitting in an old straight back wooden chair. He had it leaned against the outside of the grist mill wall next to the door. When I got to where Mr. Winslow was sitting, I could tell he had his eyes closed. He looked like he was snoozin' the way he did the day he fed us cornbread and syrup.

"Hidey, Mr. Winslow," was my greeting. The old man opened his eyes and nodded at me. He then picked up a forked stick laying next to his chair, took a 'nife from his pocket, and started carving on the stick.

"What ya doin'?" I asked. "Jes' whittlin'," he said. "May make a slingshot stock for Willie if'n this hickory stick pans out."

"Where is Willie?" was my next question.

"He's home with his granny," he said. "She's ailin' real bad today. Can't work or nothin' like she's been doin' all her eighty sumpin' years. I mighty worried 'bout her dees days. Don't know if she'll make it much longer. Jes' her and Willie, ya know. Willie got to stay close by case she needs sumpin'."

Mr. Winslow kept whittling while I was standing there trying to decide what to do next.

"I'll hep you shuck and grind your corn," I offered.

"Ain't got no corn to grind," he replied. "Folks done jes' 'bout quit bringin' corn. All last year's corn 'bout gone by now. This year's corn airn't ready yet fer month or more."

As I started to leave, Mr. Winslow stopped whittling for a minute. He looked off into the distance and started reciting a little rhyme that seemed very familiar to him. From the rhyme he appeared to gain some special satisfaction. With a big comfortable look on his face, he said, for no apparent reason, "A naught's a naught, a figger's a figger, it's all fer de white man, none fer de nigger."

"No, you can't use a word like that," I yelled, showing the same reaction I did with Skeeter when we first met and he had used that word. "My daddy said that's a vile word and shouldn't never be used."

"Cool down," he said. "Yo daddy's right, tho' I mus' say I didn't know any white folks 'round here cared nothin' 'bout black folks' feelings. But don't worry yo' sef, it don't mean de same when I say it."

More confusion in my mind. I started walking back down the dirt road. As I walked, I wondered how I was to ever make sense of what I was learning. I again felt like King Solomon had said about his getting smarter made him worry more.

I was especially curious how folks around here recited things out loud, the way that Mr. Winslow just did, that don't seem to mean nothin' to nobody but them. Like Mr. Taylor down at his store. Everytime one of the old men hanging around his store didn't agree with something Mr. Taylor said, he'd rear back, chuckle, and say, "Well, you can't teach a pig to sing. It takes too much time and annoys the pig." Then he'd go, "Ha Ha Ha," real loud.

And there was another man just like that who came in Mr. Taylor's store sometimes when I was there. He was real tall and skinny. He wores cowboy boots, grinned all the time, and spat tobacco juice in Mr. Taylor's trash can, which made Mr. Taylor angry.

Anyhow, this tall feller just loved to bust in the store when somethin' good had happened to him and say out real loud, so everbody could hear, "I tell ya, boys, the sun don't shine in the same dog's ass always. Either the dog moves or the sun does." Then he went "Ha Ha Ha," and the other men laughed with him. What got me was they all laughed every time he said that, like they hadn't heard it before. I s'pose when I get older I'll come up with sumpin' that tickles my funny bone like that.

Going back down the dirt road toward home wasn't near as much fun as it was when I was headed up toward the grist mill looking forward to seein' Willie and maybe Skeeter.

Walking along the road, I figured that life wasn't much fun with nobody interesting to talk to and nary a thing to do. My spirits were lifted by the curiosity of what might be behind the picket fence along a short stretch of the road. I had been ignoring the fence entirely on previous trips past due to my interest in other adventures. Today was different.

I got over the shallow ditch between the road and the fence. I pulled myself up to the picket fence, but I found I was unable to see over. I then wedged my face in the narrow space between two of the boards of the fence and began my survey of the premises behind. My attention was caught by the presence of an old unpainted small wooden house with a tin roof at the back of the property. The house had a front porch like our back porch with a tin roof. The whole front yard and the side yard as well was filled completely over with a garden. In that part of the garden next to the side of the house, I saw an old man in bib overalls. He had on a straw hat and was stooping over, thumping watermelons.

I watched for a while, then hollered, "Hey there, whatja doin?"

The old man stood up, took off his hat, wiped his face with a big red handkerchief that he took from his pocket, and looked for the source of the question. "Over here," I hollered again. He spotted my face wedged between the fence boards and smiled. Knowing I had his attention, I asked again, "Whatja doin'?"

"Well, I'm checkin' these melons to see if they're ripe," he replied. "How you know they ripe by thumping on 'em like that?" I asked. "It's a matter of sound," the old man said. "Lift the latch on the gate there and come on in. I'll show you how it works." No sooner said than done. I was on my way through the gate, thinking, *This ain't Skeeter or Willie, but I'll talk to anything "including scarecrows,"* or so says my momma.

It weren't more'n a matter of minutes 'fore I was a world champion watermelon thumper. The old man kept coaching me like we were gettin' ready for some championship match of some kind. "Remember now," he would say, "thump hard and listen to the sound. If it sounds hollow, that means the heart of the watermelon has done got ripe and let go of its hold on the rind." I kept thumpin' and thinkin', *I finally know sumpin' even Willie probably don't know.*

After I'd thumped so many watermelons my finger was sore. The old man said, "Thump out the best one, bring it to the porch, and we'll see how it tastes." I already had the best one picked out. Big and green, it looked to me like a winner. The old man showed me how to break the vine off the tail end of the watermelon. Then I wrestled the melon to my chest, toted it over to his porch that he was pointing to, and carefully laid it down. After brushing off some of the dirt that had rubbed off the melon on to the front of my overalls, I turned to face the old man beside me.

"I'm Ledbetter," he said reaching out his hand. "Calvin Ledbetter. Glad to meet ya."

"I'm—"

"I know you," he interrupted. "You're the preacher's boy. I go to church every Sunday if it ain't rainin' and my rhumatism ain't actin' up. They call you Junior," he contin-

69

ued. "I see you every time I'm at church. Yo' folks keeps a good eye on you, as well they should." That worried me a little.

The watermelon was delicious, to say the least. As we ate and talked, I thought about how the watermelon was as good as the cornbread soppin' I'd had with Willie and Mr. Winslow. Then I wondered if the activity before eating both had anything to do with the taste.

We finished every bit of the watermelon, spitting all the seeds out in one little pile. Mr. Ledbetter said he wanted to save the seeds out of the watermelon that I had picked. He said it looked like a 'prize' melon to him. He went on to explain how he would scatter the seeds out, let them dry, and then put them in a jar for holding till next spring's planting.

Mr. Ledbetter was a tall man. Even taller 'n Daddy and 'bout as thin. He said he had retired from his railroad job right after the war ended. He lived by himself in that small wood frame house since his wife died three years ago. He had a way of smiling as he talks that made me feel as if I could stay and listen forever. He told me he didn't have much of anybody left but him. He said his only child was a son who had been killed in the war at a place called Normandy.

Mr. Ledbetter got up and went inside his house, after saying, "Wait here a minute." When he came back out on the porch, he showed me a book full of pictures. There were pictures of him and his wife. There were also pictures of his son in his Army suit. He talked on about both of them and some others in the book. I noticed he had tears on his face the way some old ladies at church do when certain songs like "Amazin' Grace" are sung. I was beginning to get a little uneasy, so I said I needed to go. Feeling other people's pain can be a blessing or a curse. Either way, it makes me want to move on to something else.

I just couldn't bring myself to leave without showing my curiosity about the Klan rally again. "Heard anything 'bout a Klan rally with a Grand Wizard?" I asked.

"Can't imagine why you'd be interested in those folks," he replied. "Everybody's speculatin' 'bout when and where, while wishing they'd go elsewhere. But, to satisfy your curiosity, I can tell you this. I don't know the when, but the where is right over yonder in ol' man Beasley's cow pasture," he said, pointing northeast, away from town, toward the river.

I must have grinned like that Sherlock Holmes fellow when he discovered a clue. Pursuing the clue, I went further. " 'Xactly where is ol' man Beasley's cow pasture?" I asked.

"They's two ways you can get there," he answered. "First, you can go into town, get on Main Street, which is Highway 103. Follow that highway across the bridge over the river. Stay on the highway, which runs along the other side of the river. Two or three miles up the highway, after you cross the bridge, you'll see a big red barn on the left. Just past the barn on the same side is the gate to the Beasley pasture."

"What's the other way?" I asked.

"That's a little easier if you walk good," he said. "You just follow the dirt road there back up toward the grist mill. Then on past the grist mill a little ways to where the dirt road crosses the railroad tracks. Walk the railroad tracks to the trestle that goes over the river. The river ain't very wide where the railroad crosses. Just over the river on the left is a big open field Ol' Beasley uses for his cows to graze."

"Not meaning to rush off," I said, "but since I got time and I'm full of watermelon and I like to walk railroad tracks, I think I'll go look at the river by the trestle."

"Be careful," he said as I started to leave. "And by the

71

way, you know tomorrow is July Fourth, so tell your daddy to come get some good ripe watermelons to celebrate with."

"Okay," I yelled back, already well on my way toward the railroad tracks.

Walkin' railroad tracks is fun and easy. You just step from cross-tie to the next cross-tie. You don't even have to step on the rocks, called "slag," they put down all along inside the cross-ties and out on both sides of the tracks. The old men at the store explained how the slag was put down by the railroad people to keep the sparks from trains settin' fire to grass and weeds that would grow were it not for the slag. Bein' barefooted, I did have to worry 'bout splinters from the cross-ties. They could get in my feet 'cept by now my feet were tougher than most splinters.

I didn't have to worry 'bout trains neither. Only two came through every day. One came early in the morning going from east to west, Atlanta to Birmingham. Then one right after dark going from west to east, back from Birmingham to Atlanta. Nothing to do but skip from cross-tie to cross-tie till I got to the trestle which I did real soon. The railroad across the river trestle wasn't very long. Shorter'n from my house to Mr. Taylor's store. So I kept hittin' the cross-ties till I was over the river standing on the tracks, gazing out over Ol' Man Beasley's cow pasture. I couldn't see nothin' but acres of grass, lots of all colors of cows, and enough piles of cow dung to build a good-sized hill.

I did see a barbed-wire fence with three strands of barbed wire strung all around the pasture. I figured my plans for gettin' into the Klan rally, if it ever got here, might necessitate gettin' through that fence. If I didn't ever find out the Klan's code word and handshake.

Sun was goin' down and I'd better start home. But first I had to stop in the middle of the railroad trestle and drop some slags I'd collected into the swirling muddy water below.

ELEVEN

July Fourth wasn't no big deal at our house that year. To begin with, it started stormin' like crazy during the night. It only got worse after breakfast while I watched from the back porch. When it rained hard in this little town nestled between a river and a creek, people hereabouts tended to get more worried than in other places when it rained.

The old men down at Mr. Taylor's store always started talkin' 'bout what happened in '29 every time a cloud came up. I figured it must have been real bad in '29. They said the river and the creek met up in the middle of the town when it rained four days straight in '29. One old man told about finding his house downstream in another county. Another said his neighbor was washed away with his mule and chickens.

The rain had been comin' down all day and I was startin' to wonder if the river and creek were meetin' up again. When it rained this hard, wasn't no leaving the house for anything. Sittin' on the porch watchin' it come down outside and running off the tin roof of our back porch was all we could do. No firecrackers as planned. No parade, not even a chance to go get the watermelons that Mr. Ledbetter said we could get. Nothin' but rain, thunder, and lightning flashes that would scare the daylights out of everybody in town except those in the cemetery.

Days like this wasn't good for nothin' but thinkin' and good conversation if you had someone to talk to. Momma and Sister didn't make good sense to me when we talked. I waited to see what Daddy'd have to say when he stopped readin' and came out to the porch. Daddy had a small table and chair in the corner of our living room he called his "study." Daddy spent a whole lot of time in his study. He read the Bible and all kinds of books and newspapers when he got them. No newspapers today. Nothing was moving outside.

Daddy came out on the back porch where I was still sitting. He sat down and started watching it rain with me. By now I had a whole new bunch of questions. Before I could get the first one out, Daddy told me about a letter he just read from the state Baptist office. The letter, he said, informed him of the fact that one of the best-known Baptist missionaries was home on leave from his mission work. Daddy went on to say how this missionary was going to be in our church Sunday night to tell everybody about the mission work he had been doing for many years in Africa. Daddy said Africa was mostly all black folks. This missionary was over there, helping them build churches. My hearing those last few words about black folks and churches touched a nerve. I immediately figured this to be a sign to me from God. I figured God was sending this missionary to our church so me and Him could get things straightened out so Willie could join me in our next revival. In order to test my theory about this sign bein' sent to me, I decided to further explore the matter about which people goes to what church.

I decided to start with the Jews since we had read so much about them in the Bible. "Daddy," I said. "Can Jews come to our church?"

"Of course they can," was his reply. "If they so desire, they would be welcome."

"What about Romans?" I continued.

"They'd be just as welcome," Daddy said.

"But didn't the Jews and Romans crucify the Lord?" I posed.

Daddy was getting my drift, so he set about clearing up the whole thing that was running through my mind.

"Junior," he began, "you have to understand the whole context of God's great plan to satisfy the questions of your mind. I won't try to cover every detail of His plan, as I understand it, but just remember that the Jews are God's chosen people. God guided those people through many years of trials and tribulations. He prepared them for the arrival of His Son, who would be one of them during His earthly visit. The Jewish nation is well known to all Christians, since they provided us with most of the traditional values that we cherish today. Everything you've studied in the Old Testament side of our Bible describes the way God prepared a people to accept His Son as one of their own. When His Son was not accepted by the Jews, God allowed his crucifixion at the hands of the Romans."

"What about a Chinaman? If one come to town, could he come to our church?"

"Yes," was Daddy's simple reply.

"But ain't the Chinaman's killin' our Army boys in Korea?"

Daddy grimaced a little. "I don't have all the answers you look for," he said, "but if you give it time and always seek the truth, you will someday find the answers you seek." With that, Daddy headed back in the house.

I figured I had learned enough to work on that missionary man soon as he arrived. Between us we'd probably get this all straightened out in no time.

Come Sunday night, I was ready. Front pew as usual. Couldn't even get as much from the singing of hymns as usual. Daddy got up to introduce the speaker for the evening. He talked for a while about this man he called Brother

76

Eugene Varner. He said how he had served as a missionary in "darkest Africa."

Brother Varner got up and told us all kinds of interesting things that goes on in the jungles of Africa. He even showed some funny-looking clothes that he said the Africans wear. He talked about learning their language being such a problem. He even told how he had eaten dried grasshoppers with them to show he was no better 'n them. Then, when he was finished, he asked if anyone had any questions he could answer. Takin' that as my cue from God to start makin' things right about who could and who couldn't come to our church, I stood up as tall as I could. I had never stood up before a church full of people, let alone talk. But I kept thinking how this was my chance to get things in this church headed the right direction. I cleared my throat and let out my spiel.

"Jews 'n Romans can come to this church and they crucified the Lord. Chinaman's are welcome at our church and they're killin' our Army boys in Korea. Brother Varner went plumb to Africa so he could go to church with colored folks and eat grasshoppers with them. But I couldn't bring Willie to revival. He ain't killed nobody and wouldn't dare eat a grasshopper."

Sometimes there was silence in life that's downright scary. This was one of those times. I couldn't see the people behind me, which was most of the church. I was in the front row. I could hear their breathin', which seemed louder and faster than normal. Looking at Daddy, the missionary and the choir behind them, I got several different messages from their expressions.

The missionary's smile and nod told me that he understood and agreed with everything I'd said. Daddy looked a little uneasy. Most of the choir looked horrified. I kept standing 'cause once you stand up to ask a question, you don't sit till it's answered. Seemed a mighty long time 'fore a word was spoken. I thought the whole congregation must be looking like people frozen in time.

Right before I was about to faint, a man's voice from a few rows behind me said, "Somewhere in the Scriptures I remember a verse that said 'a little child shall lead them.' " With that, Daddy and the missionary said, "Amen." Everybody stood up. Daddy said a prayer and people started leaving. As I turned to go with them, I felt a hand on my shoulder. I turned and was looking Mr. Ledbetter in the face. It was him who came to my rescue. He just smiled, looked down at me, and said, "Not everything's gonna be right in your mind for a while. Don't give up."

"No sir, I won't," was all I could mumble.

I was disappointed that my efforts had not resulted in a unanimous vote by the congregation to invite Willie in. Since that didn't happen, I decided to wait and see what new methods me and God could cook up.

The next few days just weren't the same for me and my desire to get away from the house. Seemed the rest of the family took turns watching me like a hungry dog watches a bone. I felt eyeballs on me every step I made. They also made sure I had lots to do. Momma even sat on the front porch and watched me mowing the grass for the umpteenth time. She must have thought that old push mower might turn and attack me. Every day I did the same things over and over. I'd mow, sweep, mop, and shine everything that wasn't moving in or around our house. All the time, I was wondering what Skeeter and Willie was up to. They knew where I lived and hadn't come by to check on me. Maybe they done turned on me too.

I made it through Thursday without asking a question. All I was doing was eating, sleeping, and chores. I figured I should test the situation in hopes of finding some slack in their rope.

"Daddy," I said over supper, "if y'all plan to treat me like a dog, why don't cha go ahead and tie a rope 'round my neck and tie me to the tree out front the way Mr. Huggins does his old black dog?" It has always amazed me what sympathy can do. It was unanimous in the family! Daddy, Momma, and even Sister Evelyn thought my getting Friday off to do as I pleased "within reason" was a good idea.

I later thought they might have been pleased to have me away for a while.

Friday morning and I was up and gone. I got a can of worms from the worm box that I now kept under the back porch. Within minutes I had located Skeeter and Willie on the creek bank. They were 'bout where I had found Skeeter that first time, and we set out for a good hole.

Fishin' was never so good. Long before the sun started setting, I had all the fish that I could carry on the new ten-cent stringer I had got from Mr. Taylor's store. Skeeter 'n' Willie both had all the fish they could put on their stringers, so we started for home.

Just before we got to the place where we all three goes in separate directions, Skeeter said, "You know the big Klan rally's tomorrow night at sundown."

"Heck no, I didn't know," I popped back. "Is it still gonna be in Ol' Man Beasley's cow pasture?" was my next question.

"How'd you know?" he replied.

"I got my ways of findin' out things," I assured him. Then I stopped them right there and gave them my plan.

"Now look here," I began, trying my best to sound like a real leader. "I know y'all scared and everything, but I know what I'm doin'. I'll look after ya real good." That part 'bout them bein' scared wilted them like a honeysuckle vine in the middle of a hot day.

Before they could start makin' excuses, I told them to make sure they met me on the railroad tracks where the dirt road crosses over. Be there right after sundown and I would show them exactly how we was goin' to maneuver us into that Klan rally, see the Grand Wizard and everything. I told them how I had already spent a lot of time setting up my plan. I said, "I've already walked the whole distance along the tracks over the trestle and up to the edge of the pasture. All y'all have to do is show up and follow me," I concluded.

My last instruction caused them both some uneasiness. "Make absolutely certain you bring one white pillow case," I said. "I'll take care of the rest."

"I done told my pa you wanted us to go," snapped Skeeter. "He said he don't care if'n I want to act like a fool. He also said if them Klan people found us out, they'd likely tie our hands behind us, then cut off our tallywhackers and throw us in the river." Willie cringed.

My last reminder to Willie and Skeeter as we parted ways for the day was, "Now don't dare forget. Sundown at the tracks and bring a snow white pillow case."

I got to the house long before dark. Daddy was nicer than he'd been in a while. He cleaned all the fish that I'd caught, which I didn't even know he could do. Momma fried the fish in cornmeal batter, and we all ate a meal that Daddy said was "fit for a king."

Momma enjoyed eating the fish as much as the rest of us. I swear, I believe I heard Momma saying something while she was eating that made me think she'd started seeing the good in fishing. It was hard gettin' to sleep thinking about Klannin' and wondering how I'd ever get away from the house, especially at night.

TWELVE

God looks out for folks with good plans. I believe that for sure now. No more'n we'd sat down to breakfast than Momma said she and Sister was going to a party tonight they called a baby shower. Probably wouldn't be back to the house before 9:30 or 10:00. Then Daddy piped right up 'bout a meeting at the church with the new finance committee that would keep him just as long. Glory be!

Both Momma and Daddy said something about me watching out for things around the house in their absence. I mumbled around 'bout always looking out for things around the house, being careful not to commit an outright lie.

I already had picked out an old pillow case that I figured Momma wouldn't miss if I lost it. I also pulled out an old pair of my school scissors to take along. I would use those for cutting out the eyes, nose and mouth part from the pillow cases once we met up at the tracks.

The rest of the day was spent waiting, trying not to look anxious, which could make Momma or Daddy suspicious. All day I kept walking around thinking about things. Like how life's divided into two parts—that little bitty part when somethin' good's goin' on and that great big part waitin' for somethin' good to start.

I couldn't tell which was slowest, Momma and Sister primping up getting ready to go or the sun ever goin' down behind Sand Mountain. Which reminded me of something that Mr. Winslow had said one evening when me 'n' Willie 'n him was watching it get dark while we stood outside the grist mill. He said, "The good Lord jes' takes down one lantern and hangs up another." I was hoping the good Lord wouldn't hang up a "bright lantern" tonight since moonlight wouldn't work in our favor.

Finally, after what had seemed like a year, Momma and Sister set out to the baby shower. Daddy started toward the bank where Deacon Kelly kept the church records. The finance committee met there.

I made sure both parties had turned at least one corner, then I sped out of the yard like a rocket. I couldn't possibly run any harder up the dirt road toward the railroad tracks. I could run twice as fast without shoes on and I rarely had any on. I was still picking up speed as I went by Mr. Ledbetter's house.

I was plumb out of breath when I got to the tracks. Faithful friends Willie and Skeeter were sittin' on the track rail facing each other. "Plumb fool idea," was the first comment from Skeeter. "Sho' can't believe we doin' it," was Willie's remark. "Don't worry," I assured them. "I got it all figured out."

"We gonna more'n likely wind up in the river wiff our hands tied," Skeeter kept complaining.

"Yeah and without any tallywhackers," Willie chimed in.

"Let me have your pillow cases," I said, taking the small pair of scissors from my pocket. I then explained how I had to put the pillow cases over each of them one at a time so I could spot where I needed to cut holes for eyes, ears, nose, and mouth.

"Don't get all de way crazy," Willie said. "If'n you cuts dat many holes, dey won't be much piller case leff and dem Klan boys'll see who we is."

82

"Good point," I said. Besides, I didn't want to dawdle too long with the alterations of the pillow cases.

" How 'bout if I just cut two little eye holes 'n' see if that works?" They agreed, so I put Skeeter's pillow case down over his body till the top was touching his head. By putting spit on my finger, I applied two wet spots where I felt his eyes. We took the pillow case off Skeeter. I cut two little eye holes around the wet spots, and Skeeter put it back on. "Jes' right" he said, so I started on Willie.

Willie was taller'n me, which might have caused me to miss his eyes when I applied the spit on my finger to make the wet spot. Anyhow, when we got the pillow case back over Willie after I'd cut the two little eye holes, he acted real mad. "I can't see out dem two holes. Dey's way 'part no-where near my eyeballs. A big goggle-eyed fish wouldn't have eyeballs fer 'nuff apart to fit dem holes."

After a brief discussion, we decided to enlarge one of the eye holes in Willie's pillow case, giving him one big eye hole to look through.

"You sho' done fixed me good," was Willie's complaint while trying on his pillow case "robe." "Now you done fixed me so's I look like one dem creatures from outer space in Skeeter's funny book."

"It'll have to do," I told Willie. "We got to get movin'. I think I already hear a big racket comin' from over by the Beasley pasture."

We put our cut-out pillow cases that we figured looked just like Klan robes under our arms and started walking toward the river.

By the time we got to the river where the railroad tracks rides the trestle over the river, it was just about dark. "Hunker down," I said. "Just stoop over like me and hop along from one cross-tie to another. Don't look down at the water, it makes you dizzy. Jes' keep hoppin' and we'll be across in a jiffy."

We were hoppin' across the trestle from cross-tie to cross-tie. Skeeter slipped and dropped his pillow case, which nearly fell into the river. He quickly snatched his pillow case back up and we kept hoppin'.

Once across the river, we immediately went down the side bank of the railroad tracks toward the ditch between the railroad and the Beasley pasture. After getting over the ditch in the dark, I led them to a little clearing in the brush that I had picked out on my previous scouting trip. We made it through the brush and found ourselves at the three-strand, barbed-wire fence surrounding the pasture. I commanded that we should pause there a while before navigatin' through or under the fence so I could "size up the situation."

We stared quietly toward the gate at the other side of the pasture. Some people in white sheets with pointy-top hats were comin' through the gate. Some pick-up trucks full of other folks in white sheets standing up in the back of the trucks were also coming through the gate. The crowd was getting bigger by the minute.

The folks in white sheets were all gathering around a big cross that looked like it was made out of logs. They started talking loud and clapping their hands. I told Skeeter and Willie, "The white-sheet folks are busy greetin' each other with them secret handshakes, so's we ought to make our move." We got through the fence, put on our white "robes," and started inching our way toward the crowd. When we got about thirty yards from the back of their circled crowd, our courage ran low, so we stopped to observe.

We wasn't real comfortable with our arms being pinned under our pillow cases next to our bodies. Willie was most uncomfortable, he said, 'cause he was bigger'n us and could hardly breathe under there. "Sides 'at," he said, "dis one eye ain't gonna be no help when dey look dis way."

We was standing as tight together as we could get. Willie in the middle, with me on one side and Skeeter on the other. We were craning our necks, trying to get the eye holes in the right place by movin' our heads. We were trying to see the Wizard.

The noise was gettin' louder and louder so we could hardly hear when we tried to whisper to each other.

The crowd had grown out to just a few yards from us when I realized a big hand was on my shoulder coming from behind. There must have been a hand put on Skeeter's shoulder at the same time 'cause I heard him say somethin'.

There we stood, Willie in the middle, not knowing me and Skeeter had hands on our shoulders. I figured we done met up with supreme danger.

The voice that came with the hands started talking. "Now who's you three fine young'uns out here with tonight?" the voice asked. He sounded like one of them tugboats that sometimes comes up river. We did not reply. The only sound comin' from us was loud heartbeats, knocking knees, and deep breathin'.

"If'n y'all don't tell me who yo pappy is, then I'll have to peek under yo' robe," he said.

We couldn't have answered had we wanted to. Our mouths and jaws were locked by fear.

"Okay then," the foghorn voice continued. "I don't like breakin' our sacred vow of secrecy by rippin' off robes, but that's all I can do when a member at the meeting don't identify hisself."

With that, the man behind us removed his hands from Skeeter's shoulder and mine, at the same time. Then he grabbed both sides of the top of Willie's pillow case and yanked if straight up, leavin' Willie standin' there big as you please.

"Good God Almighty, it's a nigger," the man yelled, sufficient to be heard by everyone within a mile.

We all three jumped as if struck by lightning, pulling off our pillow cases. Willie's was still in the big feller's hands. We shot back toward where we had come from with the big man right behind us screamin' how we was imposters.

We made our way back through the barbed wire fence with Skeeter leaving "a little of his butt on a barb," he told us later. The man who had discovered us was now joined by several others. They all headed forward, trying to catch us, yelling all kinds of nasty words about what they'd do when we were caught. I sure was glad they was wearing those robes and didn't take them off. That way I knowed they weren't gonna ever catch us.

We were back up on the railroad tracks not far from being back on the trestle. The mob was getting over, through, and under the fence.

We were runnin' hard as we could back toward the river. We were getting to the railroad trestle, with the mob just getting up to the tracks when Willie screamed as though he was shot. "Lordy, have mercy, look a yonder!" He pointed, we looked, and our hearts sank. That old train from Birmingham back to Atlanta every night was comin' straight at us.

Both Willie and Skeeter were showing their tempers and their lack of faith in my leadership abilities. I was just plain scared to death.

"When de mob gets here, we're dead or when de train gets here, we're dead," Skeeter summized. Within seconds, we had agreed to go on out on the trestle. Maybe jump into the river. "Drown fer sho'," Willie warned. Time was running out. The mob was almost to one end of the trestle and the train almost to the other. It was Skeeter's turn to show some brilliance and he did.

"Drop our pillow cases in the river," was his first command. I did and he did. The big goon still had Willie's. "Now ease yo self down between two cross-ties, wrap yo' arms around a cross-tie. Then let yo' legs dangle down and hold hard as you can. Keep yo' arms around the cross-tie."

We did exactly as Skeeter had told us and were all three holding on with our arms around a cross-tie and our legs dangling down toward the water. We were just in time for the train to start passing over us.

The mob in white robes musta thought the train knocked us all in the river. They all rushed down to the river's edge, trying to fish our dropped pillow cases from the muddy waters.

Thank God for short trains. As soon as the last car and the train's caboose had passed, we dragged ourselves back up on top of the cross-ties. We ran as hard as we could for home. The last we saw of the mob in white, they were still trying to fish our pillow cases out of the water.

I was still running hard as our house came into view. I could see I was safe by the lack of lights being on. I turned the corner into our yard, leaped to our porch, and was in my bed as quick as possible. It was a good thing I did. It was only a matter of minutes before all three of my family got home. As if they were operating as some kind of a committee, they all stuck their heads through my bedroom door to make sure of my presence. After that, I could hear them talking in the kitchen. I was surprised to hear Daddy telling them how the news got to them during their meeting about the Klan rally being cut short on account of imposters who infiltrated the rally. Whoever delivered the good news of the shortened rally to Daddy and the others in his meeting said that some young boys had been found at the fringe of the rally crowd. The Grand Wizard had figured their papas would be in there somewhere. Not wanting to reveal their plans to strangers, the Wizard had ordered the dismantling of their cross to await a more secure rally time.

Daddy concluded his account of what he'd heard about the Klan rally. He said the messenger had told them that at least two of the young infiltrators had fallen into the river trying to make their escape across the railroad trestle. They knew that 'cause two small Klan robes were fished from the river.

The good news to Daddy was the rally being canceled and the Grand Wizard promising to set up a replacement rally in a safer county. Gettin' the rally out of town seemed a major victory in Daddy's mind.

Hearing all that, I tried gettin' to sleep while wishing I could run into the kitchen and explain how me 'n' Willie 'n' Skeeter had scuttled the Klan rally.

THIRTEEN

It sure rained a lot during summertime in these parts. Storms blew in without much notice. Big black clouds settled over the valley. Lightning flashed, thunder rolled, and rain came down like it was dumped straight out of giant tubs. The good part was it blew over 'bout as fast as it blew in. The minute the rain stopped and the dark clouds moved out, I always rushed outside to look for one of those big rainbows that gave the town its name. I hadn't seen one since we got here.

All the old men who hangs around Mr. Taylor's store plus Skeeter 'n' Willie and even Mr. Ledbetter was always tellin' how seein' one of them rainbows brought good luck. Well, I kept starin' till my eyes got sore, even after all the clouds were gone and the sun was out bright and I hadn't seen nary a rainbow. Momma said I was liable to get struck by lightning 'cause I didn't wait till the storm was plumb gone 'fore I was in the yard looking for a rainbow.

Summertime lasted forever, which wasn't bad considering the alternative bein' school. It wasn't that I didn't like the learnin' part of school, it was the bein' cooped up all day that hurt. Anyhow, it was summertime and I'd make the best of it.

Momma brought me two books from the library, saying reading was a good way to occupy my time. One book was about a horse, which I read. The other book was about that feller Huckleberry I keep hearing about, but Daddy grabbed that from Momma's hand, saying he'd take it back to the library 'cause I didn't need new ideas.

Days drag by when there's nothin' much to do. I went 'bout my days, readin' a little, mostly to please Momma, looking for lucky rainbows, fishin' every chance I got and occasionally visiting the grist mill or Mr. Ledbetter.

A lot of prayin' goes on 'mongst Baptists. Daddy, Momma, and sometimes Sister Evelyn all prayed out loud in their rooms most nights. The thin walls and open doors of our house meant I hear most of what they were sayin' in their prayers. I noticed that next to God's name, my name got mentioned second most often. I whispered my prayers 'cause I wanted God to hear me but not everybody else.

As I said before, meetings of all kinds are a big part of a Baptist church. Daddy just told us about another one. This was a special called meeting of the board of deacons. Daddy said it was to, "discuss the role of our church in a changing world." *'Bout time,* I thought. The meeting was set for tonight at seven o'clock in the choir room of the church. The choir room at our church was a small area walled off behind the front of the church where the preacher stood to deliver his sermons. The choir sat up behind him. The room was there to give choir members a place to put on their robes before church began. The choir room was plenty big enough for Daddy and all seven deacons to sit in a circle. Beings how the choir room was at the back of the church, that put it in the area that was highest off the ground. That meant I could get under that part of the church housing the choir room where I could hear what went on at a board of deacons meeting.

I was under the church right under the choir room. I sat on the ground and leaned back against a pillar that supported the floor of the church. I was there by the time the meeting began.

The meeting took lots longer than I had expected. I left before it was over. I couldn't make out everything that was said. Some of the deacons talked loud enough so I could easily make out what they said. Others didn't, which left gaps in my understanding of their concerns.

From what I could get of their meeting, I could tell they were most concerned about something having to do with colored people in Birmingham. They were talking about going to white schools and things like that. It upset the deacons. They also talked about how colored people would soon be going to white churches. Just "to raise a stink," as they put it.

My name came up in their conversation. They said something 'bout how my question to the missionary when he was at our church "was not in good taste."

Daddy handled that with some words about me bein' an average boy my age, trying to work things out in my mind. One of the deacons kinda took his side. He also said something about me being an average boy like he was way back.

Talkin' 'bout me bein' average this or average that made me curious to find out exactly what average was. I decided to think about average for a while until I could find the right person to ask. I knew that person wouldn't be Daddy 'cause then he'd know that I was eavesdropping again.

Having slept on the question of what was average, I decided to go ask Mr. Ledbetter that one. I figured I had a good friend in that old man, and besides, he would offer watermelon when I showed up.

Sure enough, I found Mr. Ledbetter in his garden as usual. He was pulling weeds from amongst his tomatoes that were red and ripe. He was glad to see me and after we talked a minute, I offered my help with the weed pulling.

"Be careful not to damage the tomato plants," he cautioned as I began to work.

After pulling weeds a few minutes while exchanging idle comments about the hot weather and how glad he was the Klan rally had fizzled a few days ago, I got my chance to ask my current nagging question.

"Mr. Ledbetter," I said, "what exactly does it mean when people say somethin' is average?"

He looked at me with a curious smile, as though confused by my simple question. Then he knelt down on one knee between two rows of tomatoes. He motioned me to kneel down in front of him, which I did.

"Take your finger and draw a short line out in front of you in the dirt," was his instructions. I reached out far as I could from where I was kneeling. I drew a line in the dirt with my finger coming back toward me about one foot long.

"Good," said Mr. Ledbetter. "Now starting in front of your foot, draw a line out toward the bottom of the line you just made." Again I did as instructed, having created two lines in the dirt with my finger that almost met.

"Now," the old man said, "that top line represents the best and the bottom line represents the worst."

I said, "Yessir."

He went on to say, "The bottom of the top line is the worst of the best. The top of the bottom line is the best of the worst. Where they meet is called average." He smiled as big as if he'd just given me some magical formula. I smiled back, thanked him, and decided my question wasn't worth chasing any further.

I also thanked him for the watermelon before starting for home.

On my way home, I decided to check out whatever might be happening around Mr. Taylor's store. It was just about on my way anyhow. I was getting close to the store when I began hearing loud bangs like firecrackers. I figured somebody had firecrackers that they hadn't used on the Fourth of July with it raining so hard. I broke into a trot to make sure I got to where the bangs were coming from before they were all used up. I turned onto the plank sidewalk that went in front of the store I was just in time to hear another loud bang. I stopped cold in my tracks, seeing Mr. Taylor falling out the front door of his store face down onto the plank sidewalk. Mr. Taylor was lying there bleeding all over the planks, still holding a pistol in his hand. Another man whom I'd never seen before was standing over him, holding a pistol in his hand.

Two men who'd been hiding in the store while the shooting was going on came, easin' their way through the door, watching the man standing over Mr. Taylor with the pistol in his hand. One of the men bent over and touched Mr. Taylor's neck. The man with the pistol moved over and sat down on one of the nail kegs on the porch.

The man touching Mr. Taylor's neck raised up and said, "He's deader'n a door nail."

The man on the nail keg said, "One of y'all go call the law." With my very own eyes, I had seen a man dying.

The sheriff's car stopped at the front of the store. I left running for home, shocked and sick over what I'd seen. The next few days was filled with conversation from everyone about Mr. Taylor's death.

The man who'd shot Mr. Taylor was a fellow named Lee. People said the man named Lee showed up at the store with a gun in his hand. He started accusing Mr. Taylor of "carrying on with his wife" while he was working out of town. They both had guns and starting firing at each other. The result was Mr. Taylor's sudden demise.

They put the fellow Lee in jail, saying a trial would come up in a week or two. When I went to get a haircut, I heard the men at the barbershop talking. One said they'd probably give Lee the electric chair. Most of the other men in the barbershop said the Lee fellow wouldn't get much of anything if he proved Mr. Taylor was carrying on with his wife behind his back. In Alabama, they most likely always let a fellow off in those circumstances. They all agreed. The trial was where the truth would all come out.

FOURTEEN

The trial for Mr. Lee started the next day. I sure would have liked to go. So would everybody else in town. Daddy said he had better things to do. He also said it wouldn't look good for him to go. Besides that, he said, he just wished he could have met Mr. Lee before he committed his evil deed.

I begged Daddy to let me go with somebody else. He said I could go if I found a proper adult to go with. I figured good ol' Mr. Ledbetter needed to see me again.

I found Mr. Ledbetter sittin' on his porch as though he expected me. I explained how I didn't have much time. I told him I'd have to be home by dark. The sun was already nearing the mountaintop, so I jumped right into the purpose of my visit.

"Ever been to a trial?" I asked.

"Three or four," he replied.

"Going to Mr. Lee's trial tomorrow?"

"I hadn't planned on it."

"Well, I ain't ever been to a trial and I'm dying to go. Daddy won't go but said he'd let me go if I found a proper adult to go with."

Mr. Ledbetter explained how the courtroom would be filled. We'd have to be there early if we wanted to get in. He said for me to be on our front porch early tomorrow. He would walk over to my house so we could meet up. Then he said we'd walk on over to the courthouse in time to get a seat.

I was on our front porch early. I got a few false starts

from other people walking by that I mistook for Mr. Ledbetter. In time, Mr. Ledbetter showed up. He was dressed as if he were going to church. White starched and ironed shirt without a tie. Neatly creased khaki britches and dress shoes. The same way he dressed for church. I felt bad that I didn't know to dress up.

On our way to the courthouse, I asked a lot of questions. "What goes on in a courthouse?" I began. "Well, there's a lot that goes on with the Sheriff's office and everything else that's in there. I suppose you mean what goes on in the courtroom," he replied.

"The courtroom we're going to is a real big room that has a large table and chair at one end. The judge sits there. He has a wooden mallet on the table called a gavel. When the judge bangs the gavel on the table, people better listen."

"Yessir," I said.

He continued, "In front of the judge's table, you'll see two other tables facing him. One of those will be where the prosecutor sits."

"What's a prosecutor?" I asked.

"He's the district attorney who explains to the judge and jury what the feller did. The other table's for the defendant. In this case, that's Lee."

I assured him that I understood what he was trying to explain. We walked up the courthouse steps and entered the courtroom. The big room was already near filled. We got room for the two of us near the back.

One man was already at one of the tables facing the judge's table. Mr. Ledbetter whispered to me to say that was the district attorney. "His name is Givens," Mr. Ledbetter said. "Can't remember his first name. People say he's real pushy," he continued. "Loves to get folks convicted."

Mr. Lee came in through a door next to the judges's table. He had handcuffs on and was followed by a man in a uniform. Mr. Lee sat down at the other table facing the judge's table. Another man sat down by Mr. Lee. Mr. Ledbetter whispered to me again, "That's Lee's lawyer. His name is Watson. He's from Huntsville and one of the best." Mr. Watson was a big man and didn't look happy about being there.

Twelve white men came through the door on the other side of the judge's table. They sat down in two rows of seats off to the left of the judge's table. "That's the jury," said Mr. Ledbetter.

Right after that, the man in the uniform said something out real loud and everybody stood up. A man in a black robe came through the door and took the chair at the judge's table. "That's the judge," Mr. Ledbetter whispered again.

I said, "Yessir," but I'd already figured that out for myself.

The district attorney and Mr. Lee's lawyer went up to the judge's table. They talked real low for a few minutes. When the district attorney and Mr. Lee's lawyer went back to their tables, the judge read something out loud. After that, the district attorney walked over near the jury and began a long spiel.

"I'm here today, gentlemen, to prove that the feller at that table," pointing to Mr. Lee, "is guilty of cold-blooded murder. I am going to prove his guilt beyond any reasonable doubt," he said.

I thought that ought to be easy since Mr. Lee sat down and waited for the law after he shot Mr. Taylor. I knew that. I was there.

"I'm also going to provide a motive for his deed," the prosecutor continued. "His motive had nothing to do with his wife and Mr. Taylor, as he'd have you believe. He shot poor Mr. Taylor over a simple matter of a whiskey bill that he owed at the store."

That statement by the district attorney set the courtroom buzzin'. Some people got up to leave. The judge hit his gavel on his table. "Quiet," he said. "Quiet in this courtroom."

"Why's people leavin'?" I asked Mr. Ledbetter.

"They ain't interested in hearin' 'bout a fight over whiskey," he said. "They come here to hear 'bout lovin' and cheatin'."

The courtroom got quiet again. The district attorney continued, "Everybody here knows we live in a dry county. Bein' dry means there ain't no whiskey sold legally in this county. It's been that way for years. We hope it'll always be that way." The prosecutor took a deep breath, looked up at the ceiling, and started again. "To buy legal whiskey, you got to go fifty miles or more either direction. Mr. Taylor was a good man in many respects, but he also sold whiskey. Illegally," he said with a burst. Then he continued, "I am going to bring the source of Mr. Taylor's whiskey before you today. In the meantime, I want to prepare you for the truth. Mr. Lee's fine counsel is going to try to have you believe something about his wife and Mr. Taylor. That rumor was started in hopes of throwing this trial off course and gettin' some light sentence for the defendant. I'm tellin' you it ain't gonna work."

The district attorney stopped and looked around like he wanted to make sure everybody was listening, then started again.

"About a year ago, Mr. Taylor was runnin' low on money, so he devised a plan. He found a steady source of good moonshine from up on the mountain. He made arrangements for the shine to come in under the cover of darkness. He kept the shine in quart jars stashed out of sight. He sold that shine under the name of weed killer. When people didn't have cash, Mr. Taylor put their weed killer on their

98

charge accounts. Now, I have all the charge book copies from Mr. Taylor's store." When he said that, several men just got up from where they was and left. The judge whacked his gavel on his table three or four times. The men kept leavin'. Mr. Lee's lawyer put his head down like he was praying.

When the room was again quiet enough to hear, the prosecutor went on. "This feller Lee here," again pointing to the defendant, "went to Taylor's store for more weed killer. Mr. Taylor told him he had used up his credit and Lee got mad. Lee had already had more 'n enough weed killer for one day." (The jury smiled.) "He didn't stop though," the prosecutor said. "He kept arguing until Mr. Taylor pulled his pistol from his box by the cash register. He was just going to scare Mr. Lee off. He didn't know Mr. Lee had a pistol in his back pocket. Mr. Taylor tried to reason with Mr. Lee. That didn't work because it's hard to reason with a man who's full of moonshine and wants more. The shootin' started and here we are."

Then to put the finishing touches on his case, the prosecutor went on. "Blamin' the whole thing on some affair between Mr. Taylor going after Lee's wife is pure hogwash. That rumor was probably started by Lee's kinfolks. They know that foolin' with another man's wife is almost certain to be judged as justifiable homicide in Alabama. I would've thought they'd come up with a better story. After all, the people out where Lee lives knows that couldn't be true about his wife. That poor ol' woman's been sufferin' from the gout and couldn't carry on if she wanted to."

The judge hit the table with his gavel again. This time he said it was getting close to lunch time. He said for the jury to go to a room in the back where lunch would be brought in. Then he said that court would start up again at 2:00 P.M.

Me and Mr. Ledbetter went outside amongst the crowd

that was left. Everybody was offerin' opinions about the weed killer.

I heard one man talking loud. He said he had seen Mr. Taylor's charge books with the weed killer in them. He also said if Mr. Taylor had sold that much weed killer, there wouldn't be a weed in the county.

Other folks were talking about Mr. Lee's lawyer. They said he'd never lost a case like this. Somebody else said it would probably be his first to lose.

Me and Mr. Ledbetter went to my house at lunch. Momma fed us some vegetables that she said was brought by a church member. I urged Mr. Ledbetter along to make sure we were back at court by two. When we got back, we found plenty of room in the third row from the front. Mr. Ledbetter said, "Most of them didn't come back 'cause there wasn't any lovin' and cheatin'. The others are probably trying to see who's on the weed killer charge books."

The judge came back in. Everybody stood up again. A lot of loud talkin' went on between the judge and the two lawyers. The judge said, "Call your first witness."

The district attorney said, "Elmer Thigpen."

The feller in the uniform said, "Elmer Thigpen."

From the same door the judge had come through came a small, strange-looking man. He didn't look to me like he believed in bathing. He had on bib overalls and carried a beat-up hat. The district attorney motioned him to a chair next to the judge's table. Before he sat down, the feller in the uniform stuck out a Bible. The little man put his hand on the Bible while the uniformed man said something. After that, the little man took a seat, acting real nervous. The district attorney walked over to him and started asking him questions.

"State your name, please."

"E-E-Elmer Thigpen," he said. We could all see that he stuttered.

"Where do you live?"

"Sa-Sa-Sa-Sand Mountain," he replied.

"What's your address on Sand Mountain?"

"I-I-I ain't got no address."

"How do you get mail?" asked the prosecutor.

"I-I-I don't get mail." The judge interrupted the district attorney's next question and said something about addresses not always applying to people on the mountain.

The district attorney left the address question and went to the next.

"You make rot-gut moonshine at your place on the mountain, don't you?"

"Na-na-na, no Sir, I don't," the little feller shot back.

"You're a bald-faced liar."

Whop! The little man hit the district attorney on his nose.

The judge started banging his gavel real hard on his table. "You are in contempt of court," the judge said, looking angry. "I'm fining you one hundred dollars for that action. I'll see that you spend time in jail for anything else like that."

Elmer Thigpen reached into his overall pocket and pulled out a large roll of money. He counted out two hundred dollars and reached over, dropping it on the judge's table.

The judge said, "I fined you one hundred dollars, not two hundred."

"Ke-ke-ke-keep the other hundred, Judge. I-I-I might wanna hit 'im again," Thigpen said.

The men in the jury chuckled. The district attorney quit rubbing his nose. He then walked back to Mr. Thigpen, but he didn't get as close to him as before.

"What do you do for a living, Mr. Thigpen?" he began.

"I-I-I-I make the best whiskey on the mountain," he said.

That seemed to clear the situation in everyone's minds. Mr. Thigpen didn't want his whiskey called "rot-gut moonshine."

The district attorney knew he had everything going right. He got Mr. Thigpen to admit bringing his whiskey to Mr. Taylor's store. Just how much he didn't know. "B-b-b-been doin' it a year now," was the best he could answer. He did say Mr. Taylor paid in cash and as far as he was concerned, Mr. Taylor was a fine man.

The judge said we'd heard enough for one day. He said court would start back at ten the next morning.

Me and Mr. Ledbetter was in the courtroom early again. A smaller crowd than yesterday was ready for the finale. Before we came in, Mr. Ledbetter said, "That feller Watson is real good, but his job now ain't gonna be easy."

Lawyer Watson stood up between the judge and the jury. He was big and impressive. He spoke with a voice much like some of the evangelists who'd been to our church. We could all tell Lawyer Watson was also a fighter. Mr. Ledbetter whispered, "You can tell he's got somethin' up his sleeve by the way he's smilin'."

Sure enough, Lawyer Watson didn't even mention any carrying on between Mr. Taylor and Mr. Lee's wife. Instead, he lit right into a long spiel about Mr. Taylor bringing the whole mess on himself by fooling around with illegal whiskey. As he talked, I could tell some of the men in the jury agreed. They nodded when Lawyer Watson hit a high note. He brought in two different men whom he called character witnesses. They got in the witness chair next to the judge's table. When Lawyer Watson asked them questions, they told about how Mr. Lee was a good ol' boy.

The district attorney asked them some questions too.

102

When they answered his questions, it sounded like they also liked Mr. Taylor's weed killer.

Lawyer Watson made his last speech, looking right at the jury. He lit up in the face like a cheap light bulb. He walked up and down in front of the jury. All the time he was waving his arms and making sure everybody heard him.

"I was raised on a farm right up there on that mountain," he said, pointing westward.

Mr. Ledbetter leaned over and whispered to me, "That's a lie. His daddy was a big time politician."

Anyhow, Lawyer Watson kept going. "I can tell all of you about sowin' and reapin'. Even the Bible says 'as we sow so shall we reap.' I know from my own experience, when I planted corn, corn came up. When I planted beans, beans came up." Then he hit the big point. "Mr. Taylor planted evil and evil came up. That evil he planted came up to render his sad demise." He sat down.

The room was quiet for a while. The judge made a short talk, and the jury people left through the door they had come through. They weren't gone very long. When they got back in, they handed a note to the feller in the uniform. He read the note, but I couldn't hear.

The judge hit the table with his gavel and everybody left. When we got outside, Mr. Ledbetter explained to me that the jury had found Mr. Lee guilty of something other than murder. He said it was called manslaughter. He said that meant Mr. Lee would be out of prison in two or three years at the most.

Walking back to my house, Mr. Ledbetter said that Lawyer Watson really was one of the best. "That story 'bout sowin' and reapin' hit them ol' jury boys hard," he said. "It didn't hurt none that they'd probably tried some o' that weed killer theyselves," he concluded.

FIFTEEN

Bad things comes in bunches, Daddy always said. I'm beginning to believe it's true. First came the tragedy of Mr. Taylor. Then three or four storms that didn't leave a single rainbow that I could see. Then there were at least three trips to the fishing holes with Skeeter and Willie with barely one fish to show. Willie said it was the hot days that "had made the fish too lazy to bite."

Now came the worst news of all. A gentle knock on our front screen door sent me running to greet whoever it was. Momma and Sister were right behind me. We don't get that many visitors, especially in the heat of the day.

To my surprise, the knock on our screen door was made by Mr. Winslow. The old black gentleman was standing there in front of our door, holding his hat, with his white hair looking whiter than ever. He looked over my head and spoke to Momma standing behind me. "Jes' thought yo' boy here ought to know Willie's granny died last night," he said.

Mr. Winslow continued to speak in low tones, with obvious pain. "She wuz my last sister and I sho' gonna miss her. Willie gonna miss her, too, 'cause he ain't gone have nobody to look out fer 'im. I'm too old and can hardly look after me. Don't know what Willie gonna do. Maybe stay wit' me for now. Ain't no way I can take care o' him when school starts back. Anyhow, I jes' wanted yo' boy to know Willie won't be out an' about. Mrs. Lilly—dat's what we called her—passed in her sleep last night. We'll be burying her tomorrow, two o'clock, at Shiloh Baptist Church, jes' a little further up from the grist mill."

The old man walked slowly off our porch as we offered our condolences.

"It was as if he was asking me to be at the funeral," I said, turning back to face Momma and Sister.

"I don't think so," was Momma's reply. "I think he just wanted you to know about Willie's sorrow. He knows how you and Willie have become friends."

I went to the back porch, where I do my best thinking.

I began to wonder how I'd feel in Willie's place. Not knowing where to live or who would cook or anything. I thought maybe Willie could come live with us. Put another bed in my room and we'd do just fine. Then I remembered all the stuff bein' talked about colored folks. I figured that would stir up a bigger ruckus than if I took him to church.

After supper, I was anxious for another of my sittings with Daddy on the back porch. He was as patient and understanding as I had expected him to be. We talked about dying. What makes people die. How one might feel when dying and everything else that I could think up on that subject.

Daddy knew a lot more about Willie's granny and the circumstances surrounding her health than I had expected. I had forgotten how preachers in small towns know about everything.

"After all," he said, "she was in her eighties. From what I hear, she lived a godly life. Willie was her only grandchild and she loved him dearly. She is already amongst the angels in heaven," was Daddy's concluding remark. I could just see her now in my mind, already sprouting wings.

As we started in to the house from the porch, I told Daddy of my desire to attend the funeral of Willie's granny tomorrow.

Daddy placed his arm around my shoulder and said, "I thought you would and I'll go with you." That's all I needed to make my night most restful.

Funeral days are the worst of all days, especially when it rains. It rained all morning, but it started clearing up close to noonday. Daddy put on his best suit that he saves for weddings and funerals. My one suit was way too little for me now. I put on my only pair of blue jeans. I also put on my shoes with white socks. Daddy said it would be disrespectful to go barefooted for anyone who had shoes. My white, short-sleeved dress shirt completed my attire for the funeral. I had to leave it unbuttoned at the neck to keep from choking.

Me and Daddy left the house with plenty of time to walk the dirt road past Mr. Ledbetter's place. Then on past the grist mill, finally arriving in the yard of the Shiloh Church before the funeral service began. The churchyard was full of people and several wagons pulled by mules. Their drivers had tied them to the fence separating the church yard from the cemetery.

Daddy took off his hat as we entered the church yard. He was sweating something awful from the hot day and long walk.

People were standing quietly talking in low voices. They all spoke or nodded as we passed slowly toward the front door of the church. We spoke and nodded back.

I located Willie standing next to his Uncle Winslow and another black gentleman. They were at the steps leading up to the door of the small white wooden church. A simple sign over the church door said: "Welcome to Shiloh Baptist Church." Underneath those words was the number 1889, which I took to be when the church started.

Willie had on a brand new pair of overalls but no shoes. I took that to mean he didn't have any shoes. The man

106

standing with Willie and his Uncle Winslow stuck out his hand to me and Daddy. He said he was glad to see us and said his name was Pastor Amos Walker. Greetings completed, we stood silent for a few minutes, with me trying to tell Willie how bad I felt for him with my expression.

When the men started talking again, Willie asked me if I'd like to go in and meet his granny. I nodded yes, thinking he made it sound like she'd be sitting up ready to talk.

Me and Willie walked together down the church aisle between the two sides filled with benches. We stopped at a wooden casket sitting on top of a long table at the front of the church.

Willie and me stood close together side by side as we stared down at the elderly lady in the casket. We didn't say nothing for a while and I could see tears on Willie's face. "Dear Sweet Granny," was all he could get said, "sho' gonna miss you." I felt like I was gonna bust for the lack of something to say. I felt like I was chokin' on something.

Things got a little better when Willie started telling how he helped his Uncle Winslow and a neighbor cut the pine boards and nail them together to make the casket. He then told how they used his granny's best quilt she'd made to line the casket. They had folded the quilt so half fit the bottom of the casket where she lay. The other end was draped over the side to be folded back over her body for burial.

Willie showed how they put her best pillow under her head. That made it look to me like his granny was just lying there taking a nap. She was dressed in a snow-white dress that matched her white hair and the white pillow where her head lay. I couldn't take no more. Before I busted out weeping for Willie and his granny, I turned around trying to say how sorry I felt. Then I eased back to the door where all the people were starting to file in.

Me and Daddy seated ourselves in a pew near the back.

We didn't want to prevent a close friend or family member from being nearer the deceased during the funeral service.

Pastor Walker said a long beautiful prayer followed by a sermon about living and dying. It was sufficient to make tears in the eyes of marble statues.

The preacher's sermon was about death. He said people shouldn't get so sad when other people die. He said when we die, our soul goes to heaven and our body just rests till judgement day. He read a poem that he said was written by someone called "Nonomus."

" 'I wish I was a little stone, a sittin' on a hill,
I wouldn't think, I wouldn't move, I'd be so very still.
I wouldn't laugh, I wouldn't cry, I wouldn't even smile,
I'd just sit a thousand years and rest myself a while.' "

When the preacher finished reading his poem, he looked at the teary-eyed congregation and said, "This dear lady is merely restin'."

They didn't have any musical instruments in the church, like a piano or organ. They sang a few songs without any music help. After they started singing, I knew why they didn't have musical instruments. They didn't need any. From the way they sang their songs, I figured they wouldn't even need any of those golden harps that they say will be in heaven. I bit on my lower lip. I pinched hard on my leg and even considered gouging my finger in my eye as a last resort. That way I could at least explain my tears if I didn't hold them back.

My situation worsened when the congregation stood up to sing the last hymn selected for the funeral service. The hymn they sang was "Amazin' Grace." That hymn seems to be everybody's favorite song to sing in church. I've been hearing and singing that song on a regular basis for as long as I can remember. The words and the melody seem to strike some special nerve in the heart of everybody who hears it.

Daddy told me how "Amazin' Grace" was written by a feller from England long before the Civil War. His name was John Newton. He started out being Captain John Newton, who was a master on sailing ships. His ship was hired out to haul slaves from Africa to places in the South where they had to pick cotton. I felt like I could almost see that feller Newton in my mind when Daddy said he might have sailed a ship full of slaves to Alabama.

Anyhow, Daddy said the sight of all those slaves stashed into the little rooms on John Newton's ship caused a great change to come over him. Captain John Newton became Preacher John Newton. After writing that song, he went back to England. He became a preacher and spent the rest of his life preaching against slavery and all other bad things people do to each other. I figure the way that song pulls on people's hearts is God's way of letting those slaves remind us of the evil deeds of our ancestors.

The funeral service ended. Some men sitting in the front row gently folded the outside half of the quilt over Willie's granny. Then they placed the top over the casket. After that, they divided up on both sides of the casket and carried it out to the cemetery. Me and Daddy stood at the back of the crowd gathered at the grave site. We waited with heads bowed till that part ended. Somebody up near the grave site said, "Amen," and the people started leaving. I wanted to say something else to Willie, but he had lots of folks around him. Me and Daddy headed out of the cemetery toward home.

I kept feeling bad for Willie all the way home, but I didn't say nothing to Daddy. We just walked along back toward the house while the sun was starting to get down just above the top of Sand Mountain.

SIXTEEN

Some days just ain't as good as others for reasons I can't understand. I got up the next day feeling worse than I had ever felt without bein' sick. I figured it had a lot to do with my dreams the previous night. I don't always dream at night. I did that night. The dream I had musta lasted all night the way I felt then. I kept dreamin' how's everybody I knowed was dead. They were all lying in wooden caskets, settin' on tables, like Willie's granny. I was runnin' 'round squalling my eyes out over and over as the dream kept repeating itself. Now I was up like I always was that time of day, but I felt like I was still half dreamin' and half awake. I didn't like that feeling. I figured I needed some answers to important questions to make everything all right. I ate a quick small breakfast. Then I set out to make this day a time for some answers to my questions.

Dealing with death ain't easy for nobody. Especially the first time. Up until my seeing Mr. Taylor lying there dying on the wood sidewalk in front of his store and Willie's granny at the funeral, I hadn't seen death up close. There was that one time I went to Aunt Sara's funeral. I was much younger then. I hadn't known Aunt Sara hardly at all. She was old and lived in a place with old folks. Going to her funeral hadn't caused me to feel any pain.

Now it was different. I didn't know why, but something was gnawing at my insides. It made me want to get things straight in my mind.

I decided to begin my quest for understanding more

about death at the spot of my first exposure. Mr. Taylor's store. On my way to the store, I thought how Skeeter and Willie might be hangin' around down there. Then I remembered how Skeeter don't talk about nothin' that ain't fun and hates questions of any kind. No wonder he's still in third grade. He probably gets mad every time his teacher asks him anything.

I walked up to the plank sidewalk in front of the store. I tippy-toed on up close to the spot where Mr. Taylor had died. I stopped right beside where I had first seen him lying there gushing blood. I stared in silence at the place where he had lain. I felt even worse seeing the blood stains still on the planks of the sidewalk. How sad it seemed that somebody could be alive one minute and dead the next. I remembered what the lawyer had said about sowin' and reapin' at the trial. I still missed seein' Mr. Taylor.

I felt like any minute now Mr. Taylor would swing open the door to his store and invite me in to smell the candy. I caught myself thinking how good it was that the only things I remembered about Mr. Taylor were the good things he said and did. Like the morning I was starin' at the candy bars in his candy case with only eight cents in my pocket. I remember he said to me, "You dying for one of them Baby Ruth bars, ain't ja?"

I said, "Yessir, but I ain't got a dime. I got a nickel and three pennies."

He said, "You gimme your eight cents, I'll give you the candy. You can make up the difference later. We'll put the two cents you're short on your credit account."

I felt good about that. Not only did I get the candy, I also got some trust about paying him back. "You want me to sign one of them little slips of paper like the men do here when they get something when they ain't got money?" I asked.

111

He and the men in the store laughed. Mr. Taylor said, "That won't be necessary." Now he's gone forever and I ain't got no idea who'll eat up the candy bars left in his store.

The more I thought, the more miserable I got. Just like King Solomon again in the Book of Ecclesiastes.

I walked back to our house and sat down on the back porch. That was still the best place that I knew of for thinking. The frogs and crickets weren't making any sounds of any kind. Daddy had told me a long time ago that frogs and crickets don't sing much in the middle of the day. They're busy looking for food or sleepin'. They come out at night and make all that racket "as their way of courtin' their mates." I thought about how that was a lot like that place on the edge of town that Daddy didn't like. That was where lots of pick-up trucks parked at night and played loud music.

I was still sitting on our back porch when Daddy got back from visiting the shut-ins. He came out to check on me. "What's bothering you, Junior?" he asked. Calling me "Junior" instead of "Son" like he usually did let me know he'd talk to me man to man.

"I'm thinkin' 'bout dead people," I said. "I need some answers and I'd like to get them soon. I don't have all day. I want to get things worked out in my mind so's I can get back to doin' other things."

"Hold on now," Daddy began. "Answers to big questions like yours have never come so easy. Remember how I've always told you questions about our lives and our death must find answers from within God's master plan?"

"Well, that may be easy for you," I replied, "but I can't see why God don't jest tell me Hisself like He did for some of the prophets you read about."

Seeming a little short of time but not wanting to dampen my desire for answers, Daddy tried again. "Just keep in mind what I've told you before. One of the most pro-

112

found aspects of all human beings is our desire for tangible answers. Don't forget, God wants you to find the answers that you seek through faith and patience. Sometimes I get depressed when I realize how folks look to preachers, priests, rabbis, and other church leaders as having all the answers. We should be seen as individuals leading our flock in search of answers. For your own sake," Daddy continued, "God is not going to hand you a set of answers to your questions. For Him to do so would destroy the opportunity for you to grow the faith and love in Him that you need. You keep thinking and we'll talk again later," he said, leaving the porch.

I figured that I'd give God all the help I could in figuring this mess out. I would start where He started, at the beginning. I was thinking slow and clear now. God created man, woman, and the whole world in six days. Just like it says in the first book of the Bible, called Genesis.

I had to stop that line of thought momentarily in order to insert another idea that I'd picked up during a third-grade classroom discussion. In that class our teacher had talked about how some real smart people called scientists had figured out that people come from something called the process of evolutin'.

The scientists said it took a zillion years and we all came from monkeys. Sometime after that third-grade class back in Shady Grove, Daddy had took us to the zoo in Birmingham. Soon as I got to the zoo, I went to the monkey cage. I looked at them for a long time. I did see some resemblance to the monkeys. I also thought Sister Evelyn resembled the monkeys more'n I did.

Anyhow, even if the real smart scientist people said we come from monkeys, I'll stick to the God story. The reason for that is in something I feel. I believe that if I'd of dropped dead in front of those monkeys I looked at, they wouldn't of

113

felt nothin'. They'd of gone right on, eatin' their peanuts that people throwed them. But if one of them would've dropped dead, I would've felt real bad. That feeling makes me believe God put something in humans that other beings didn't get.

Besides that, if there was anything to that process of evolutin', the monkeys would have evolved out of their pitiful state of affairs by now. They been around long as we have and they must not be too happy 'bout standing around waving their arms to get people to toss peanuts to them.

I then decided to put it all aside till after lunch. Then I would think some more and finish it all off with Daddy on the porch tonight.

I spent an afternoon of thinking, interrupted only by the coming and going of birds in our backyard. Then a big supper, after which I was ready for another back-porch session with Daddy.

"You got it figured out yet?" Daddy began as we sat down. "I got the part 'bout how we got here," I replied. "The part 'bout our leavin' ain't settled yet."

"Just remember what I've told you," Daddy said. "I cannot provide your answers. Only God can do that, and He will if you cooperate fully. Your searching for the right answers will determine the kind of person you will be on earth. The level of correctness to the answers you get will determine the condition of your soul in the hereafter. Continue your search with one important Scripture in mind: 'The Lord giveth and the Lord taketh away. Blessed be the name of the Lord.' "

I guessed we'd said all I could handle for now, so I'd just do as Daddy suggested and be patient. After all, dying might not be so bad. If what they said was true, it could turn out just fine. Dying was a one-way ticket to heaven.

SEVENTEEN

Old habits are hard to change. Me 'n Willie 'n Skeeter still met up whenever we could down at Mr. Taylor's old store. The store was closed now. Somebody nailed boards over the windows. They also put a big lock on the door and a sign that said "Closed till further notice."

Even so, we still met up there some mornings and laid out plans the way we'd been doin'. The nail kegs were still sittin' under the porch of the store on the plank sidewalk like always. We sat on the kegs and sometimes I showed Willie 'n' Skeeter just how that feller Lee was standing over Mr. Taylor, holding his pistol, when I got there. The blood I seen coming out of Mr. Taylor was still plain to see on the planks of the porch. Looking at the blood stains gave us all an eerie feeling that caused us to speak in a low tone of voice.

Some of the old men who used to hang around the store would occasionally drive up in their pick-ups. They would sometimes park their trucks, get out, and lean against their truck starin' at the store as if they expected Mr. Taylor to walk out the door.

People I met, except Willie and Skeeter, seemed to be changing in some way that wasn't for the better. Seemed all I heard outta grown-up folks was bad. Some court in another state had just passed on something to do with whites and blacks. It was called Brown versus somethin' that's made people edgy.

At the barbershop and everywhere else I went, most of

what I heard about was how black people were talking about showing up at a white school or a white church. All that seemed to bother some folks real bad. I thought it sounded pretty good. I figured God was still working on that deal about me gettin' Willie to our church.

Makin' my morning rounds, I didn't find Skeeter nor Willie at the closed-up store. I walked on up to Mr. Ledbetter's place, but he wasn't where I could see him. I walked on up to the grist mill and found Mr. Winslow fixin' the door. Willie had gone to fetch some nails to help with the door, so I decided to visit Mr. Winslow.

We talked about several things before I got around to telling him how I was hoping to work things out for Willie before school started back. I told him how I was gonna ask Daddy about putting another cot bed like mine in my room for Willie to sleep. I told him how I thought our living in my house would help us both. Then I told him how all that would make it easy for me to have Willie in our church by next revival time.

Then I discovered Mr. Winslow was getting edgy like everybody else in town. He turned around toward me and said, "Look, you may's well quit fretting yo' self 'bout Willie goin' to church wit' you. The Lawd Hisself been trying to get in dat church for years and ain't made it. Don't know why you'd try to get Willie in now." Mr. Winslow had always seemed happy and easy going. He sounded a little irritated. Maybe the colored folks were gettin' tired of hearing 'bout all the trouble that was s'posed to be brewing.

Walking back home, I noticed the sun got down even with the top of Sand Mountain sooner than it did when we first got here. School wasn't long off from starting back. School wasn't gonna be as much fun this year. I done learned too much to be locked up inside all day.

By the time I got home, I was ready for supper. Then a

little time on the back porch with Daddy talking and listening to the frogs and crickets. Over supper I could tell Daddy was worried. I didn't say nothing, but finally Daddy said they'd be another meeting of the deacons over at the church.

"In the choir room?" I asked, almost giving away my secret.

"Yes," was his only reply.

Soon as I figured the meeting was about to start, I left Momma with Sister in the kitchen. I made my way quickly to the spot under the church directly beneath the choir room. There I could hear most of what went on in the meeting, as I had done before.

As soon as the meeting started, I could tell it was not going to be in the same friendly atmosphere as the last one. One voice I could hardly make out talked first about how bad a recent court ruling had been for white and colored. Then another voice, which I recognized as Mr. Wilson, who owns a big farm north of town, started speaking.

"What we need in this here church is a solid plan to protect us against unwanted intrusions," he stated. I figured Mr. Wilson would be one to force any issue. He was one of those people you knew liked a fight the minute you saw him. He did come to church most Sundays with his little frail wife and three big boys who looked like him. His boys always looked mad about something, the same as their daddy. One day while eating watermelon, Mr. Ledbetter made a comment about how "those boys of Wilson's look like they just broke outta jail!"

After Mr. Wilson rambled on for a while about how we shouldn't wait till trouble started like it already had in Birmingham before the church decided on a plan to handle problems of that kind.

"Exactly what kind of plan do you have in mind, Brother Wilson?" Daddy asked.

"Well, let me put it to you this way, Preacher. What do you plan to do if you look up and see a bunch of big black people comin' into our church, huh?"

Daddy paused before answering, choosing his words well as he always does on something important.

"I would meet them at the door. I would extend my hand of Christian fellowship and invite them to be seated. I would then preach the same sermon that I offer to everyone who enters our church. I would act no different in any way than I would under any other circumstances. I consider my calling from God to be for me to deliver the Gospel of our Lord and Savior to anyone willing to listen. I hope to do that in a fashion that will somehow bring the joy of our Lord to their hearts," Daddy paused again, then concluded his remarks. "The peace you seek cannot be found in plans of any kind except the plan of God's not yet fully recognized by us. Until we know every detail of God's great plan, my efforts will be directed toward preaching the Gospel to all who will listen."

I could tell Daddy's response was not what Mr. Wilson and at least two others wanted to hear. More conversation followed, with each participant trying to make their particular point without seeming to condemn another. But in the end, it was made clear that Mr. Wilson would assume the role of protecting the interests of the church regarding uninvited visitors. It seemed they were about to leave the meeting with acceptable differences of opinion until Mr. Wilson put forth his final decree. "Now look here," he began in a voice showing anger. "I'm gonna make up a letter for everybody to sign stating how we don't want nobody in our church that we ain't invited. I'm gonna pass that letter around church for everybody to read and sign. That means you, too, Preacher," was his final comment as he left the room.

Things weren't good as they used to be. Daddy was looking more worried now. He don't seem to notice me, the crickets, nor the frogs when we're on the back porch.

Everybody around seemed to fit into one of three different groups of thinkers these days. The big group was led by Mr. Wilson and they wanted to put up some kind of fence between us and everybody else. Another group was like Daddy and wished to handle such matters in a dignified Christian way. Then there was folks like me who wondered what the fuss was about.

Daddy always said, "Just take one day at a time, have faith and everything will be just fine." That's what I was doing today, this next to the last Sunday before school started back. I went to Sunday school, then took my usual place on the front row ready for Daddy's sermon.

After songs were sung and everybody in the church was settled into their places ready to receive Daddy's sermon, he stepped up to the pulpit. He had an unusually relaxed look on his face as he began to speak.

"My sermon today will be brief. In fact, you might want to consider today's sermon as more of a statement regarding Christian principles. I'm saddened today by the fact that during my time in your midst I've not been able to persuade everyone of the value of placing God's love over any earthly emotions. I'm further saddened by the fact that changes around us have set off a chain of events that is destined to result in discord among our people. You remember a great book written by a lady in Atlanta, Georgia. In that book, Margaret Mitchell clearly portrayed the lives of people in the South before, during, and after that terrible Civil War. She wrote with such elegance about the wonderful lifestyles of the genteel South before the Civil War began. She described with such clarity the failure of those who enjoyed the great luxuries of that era to recognize their need to accept change. The elite of that day steadfastly refused to consider change. Their refusal led to their lifestyles being 'gone with the wind.'

"My dear people," he continued. "I have prayed so hard that hearts of Christians all over this land would be persuaded to see the need for social change and seize the opportunity to take the lead in that effort. As Christians, we have the responsibility to lead out in all matters regarding acceptance and fairness toward all human beings. As it stands today, I have to admit that, as Christians, we are forfeiting the greatest opportunity we will ever have to demonstrate to the world the true brotherhood and compassion that forms the foundation of our faith.

"By defaulting on this opportunity, we now put God in the position of finding alternatives to fulfill His will.

"I believe with all my heart His plan is being implemented as I speak. God will find the right leader to carry out the mission of bringing about the changes this nation must make if we are to continue as a nation of God.

"God will find His leader. He might find that leader from right here in Alabama. Wherever he comes from, that leader will be handpicked for God's mission.

"The leader God picks will emerge on the scene using a sword of truth, a shield of humility, and the law of the land to accomplish God's plan for all His people. Oh, how I wish that, as Christians, we could bond ourselves together to accomplish that plan.

"Not being able to do so means history forever will show that government, through its legal system, was forced to provide changes that were rightfully the responsibility of Christians. Given the situation of our times and my personal feeling of having failed this church in the brief tenure I've enjoyed, I am submitting my resignation as your pastor effective at the end of this service."

With that, Daddy said a short prayer and the service ended. People left the church quietly. Not much of anything was said.

Deacon Johnson came up to Daddy and said how he'd be happy to haul us and or belongings anywhere he could if we needed him to. Daddy accepted his offer, explaining how he was going to move us to Huntsville so he could work for a while at a college there until he found another church.

Things moved so fast that I didn't get to see hardly anybody since we were again packing all our belongings for moving. Deacon Johnson backed his truck up to our front porch so we could load up, just as we had unloaded a few months ago.

As the last of our belongings were placed in the truck, Daddy closed the door of the parsonage. We started getting into the truck to leave, sitting as we were when we arrived.

Deacon Johnson, Daddy, Momma and Sister up front. Me in the back under the tarpaulin that Deacon Johnson had pulled over the back of the truck to keep the rain out.

Before starting the truck, Deacon Johnson said he'd have to stop at the filling station to put air in a tire that looked low. He stopped his truck next to the air pump at the filling station, and Daddy let me off the back of the truck. I could "get my last look" at my latest hometown and walk around a little before beginning the long ride to Huntsville.

I walked around the back of the truck. There I was thrilled to see my friend Skeeter standing next to a pick-up truck at the gas pump. The pick-up had a house trailer attached. I was overjoyed by his presence, thinking I wouldn't get to say good-bye before we left town.

Skeeter told me that him and his pa was leaving that same day in his pa's truck. They were going back to Louisiana. He said his pa's job here was about to "peter out." They

121

wanted to make their move in time for him to start a new school year in Louisiana.

Me 'n' Skeeter was both talking at the same time like two old lost Army buddies. Then we glanced across the road to the bus station. Believe it or not, there was Willie standing with his Uncle Winslow and them both holding suitcases.

Skeeter's pa, Deacon Johnson, and my family just had to wait. I couldn't believe my luck finding Skeeter and now Willie right when I'd thought I wouldn't ever see either one again.

Me and Skeeter crossed the road. We all three jabbered and jumped around like crazy till the bus pulled up to take on new passengers.

Willie explained how his Uncle Winslow was taking him to Detroit to live with his mother. As Willie and his uncle boarded the bus, Skeeter ran back across the road and hopped into his pa's truck. I got into the back of Deacon Johnson's truck, and he pulled the tarpaulin down tight to help keep out the rain. It was starting to come down hard again.

We were starting our move right in the middle of another one of those summertime monsoon rainstorms that Alabama is so famous for getting. It had been raining off and on now for almost a full week. The man at the filling station said something 'bout all the rain we were getting and how it had already started floodin' some low-lying farms north of town. There, the river was prone to "slip over its banks at the first sign of high water." He even made a passing comment about how the Wilson boys were sand-baggin' around their house again. His comment about the Wilsons left me with a guilty smile on my face. I sure don't wish people no harm. However, I'm tickled to be reminded that God still plays "pay-back" to folks that stirs up misery for other folks.

We moved out onto Highway 103, heading back up toward the top of Sand Mountain from whence we had come at the beginning. We moved slowly up the slope of the mountain. I thought how me 'n' Skeeter 'n' Willie was going in the same order that we did when we were lost in the swamp.

Willie was leading the way in the Greyhound bus. Skeeter was right behind in his pa's truck. I was bringing up the rear in Deacon Johnson's truck.

We got up near the top of Sand Mountain about where we were when we got our first look at the town. The rain had stopped and the sun was breaking through the clouds. I raised up the edge of the tarpaulin and looked through the gap between the boards that made up the body of the truck. What I saw then gave me the thrill of my life.

The sky over the town was filled by a giant rainbow! My first lucky rainbow! It went all the way from the creek where it seemed to begin, to the river where it seemed to end.

I remembered what Mr. Ledbetter had told me one day while sitting on his porch looking for a rainbow after a summer shower. He said, "Rainbows are heavenly paintings placed by angels against the backdrop of a clear blue sky to remind us of God's everlasting love for all mankind sufficient to overcome our sorrows."

I finally could see for myself why that little town was called **Rainbow Junction.**

Epilogue

Any creation, whether art, music, poetry, or literature, that stirs kindly emotions in our souls is surely worthwhile. Should this offering provide such for even one reader, the author will have been sufficiently rewarded.